SMALL CRUELTIES

Stories by
Joanna Acevedo

Flexible Press
Minneapolis, Minnesota, 2025

The stories listed below previously appeared in the following journals, sometimes in different versions:
"The Dark Room," in Litro USA
"I Love You LIke A Brother" in *L'Esprit Literary Review* (and read aloud on *Selected Prose* podcast)
"The Grace That Comes By Violence"
in *The Write Launch*
"What Would Happen" in *Scarlet Leaf Review*

Print ISBN: 979-8-9914928-4-3
eBook ISBN: 979-8-9914928-5-0

Flexible Press LLC
Minneapolis, Minnesota
www.flexiblepub.com
Editors William E Burleson
Vicki Adang, Mark My Words Editorial Services, LLC

For Josh

Preface

SO THE THING to remember is that no one knows what they are doing and anyone who says they do is lying and probably an asshole. If you've paid them money to hear them say they know what they're doing and they can tell you how to know, too, they're a double asshole.

This is a universal truth.

When I was in college, I worked at an ice cream shop, and after work I and my (mostly underage) coworkers would buy forties of Budweiser from a deli across the street from our job and drink them in Prospect Park until we were chased out by the cops when the park closed. Then we walked around looking for somewhere to pee after drinking all that beer, and eventually we'd find a place we called "Dirty Diner." We could never find it when we were sober, but it was a deli that had a diner in the back, and they had a bathroom and cheap cheese fries.

I guess what I'm saying is that happiness is one of those things that can be a dream or it can be the way you delete your ex-boyfriend's number and then block him because he has your birthday as an alert in his phone, even five years later.

When I first started writing short stories, I wanted a way
to hide the emotions I felt in another place, so I could ex-
press them and connect with other people who felt the
same, without ever actually having to speak out loud about
anything. More often these days, I realize we are telling
each other our feelings all the time in ways we don't expect
or realize. But maybe that's the point. Maybe that's why I
love it, why I keep doing it.

Maybe I'm in love with lying, and maybe I'm in love
with telling the truth.

— Joanna Acevedo

SMALL CRUELTIES

The Ocelots

ALEX ROLLED UP on Monday with a watermelon in the front seat of his car, held in place by the seat belt.

"I'm such a good dad," he said, gesturing to the watermelon like it was his child. The sun glinted proudly off his pink hair.

I picked it up and put it in my lap as I got in the car. "What's its name?"

"Excuse you," he said, looking fondly at the melon. "This is my child we're talking about. She's not an 'it.'"

I looked at the watermelon. It was fairly average, as watermelons go. Large, oblong, green rind.

"Her name is Laverne," he told me as we drove down Arbor Street.

Laverne the watermelon rode around in the front seat for two days before she was cut up and eaten by Alex's parents on the Fourth of July. Naturally, he was horrified. I watched from his parents' porch as he drove off in a cloud of indignant smoke, then called him.

"Are you coming back to this party?" I asked.

"What party?" The sounds on the other end of the line were quiet, like the rushing of water, or maybe he was next to a highway.

"Are you coming to any party?" I shoved a fork into the plate of barbecue that rested on the porch railing.

"No," he said thoughtfully. "I'm not."

"Then why did you say that?"

I heard his laugh over the phone. "Ocelots are endangered in the U.S.," he told me. "But not in Mexico. So the border wall has special openings for the ocelots to travel through. Can you believe that, Tanya? They can go wherever they want."

"Okay," I said. "Are you going to be here anytime soon?"

"They ate Laverne," he said, and hung up the phone.

After the Laverne incident, Alex crashed on my couch for a few days while things with his parents cooled down. I could see both sides of the argument. It was an invasion of privacy, sure, but it was a watermelon. It was supposed to be eaten.

"Maybe you're being a little ridiculous," I said.

Alex could get locked in on things like this. Last winter he had gotten obsessed with snowmen and had gone on covert nighttime missions to build them in all sorts of strange places. When he got bronchitis from all the running around at night and messing around in the snow, he had refused to quit smoking and continued to steal his father's Pall Malls because he was too broke to buy his own. The snowmen had kept cropping up as Alex got sicker and sicker. When he had to be hospitalized for exhaustion and an illness that had settled in his lungs, he asked me if I could continue his mission.

"Who else will do it?" he asked me.

"Why does anyone need to do it?" I said. He refused to see me again until I built a jaunty snowman outside of his hospital window.

After that, his lungs were never really the same. I could hear his raspy breathing at night as he tossed and turned on the couch.

Alex lounged when he wasn't at work, reading his book on ocelots, which I had bought as a peace offering. Occasionally he would stop and tell me something about the animals. "Tanya," he would say, waving to get my attention. "Ocelots can mate at any time of the year."

"So? People do that too."

On the coffee table, three honeydew melons rested, each in their own knitted cozy. I hadn't asked him where he got the cozies. "Plato, Socrates, and Aristotle," he told me when I asked their names. "They seemed very thoughtful when I found them."

My friend Sketch had a new girlfriend, and before I even met her, Alex told me that he had seen naked pictures of her on the internet. "How do you know that?" I asked. I had never pictured Alex as a connoisseur of naked lady photographs. He was more interested in his book on the ocelots, his battered copy of *Plato's Republic*, the two large bags of grapefruits he had brought home after work.

When he lugged the grapefruit through the door, I hadn't asked any questions. He explained anyway.

"They were on sale," he said. "I thought it was two grapefruits, but it turned out to be two five-pound bags."

The fourteen grapefruits were too many to fit into my fruit bowl. He had finally accepted fruit as a part of a balanced diet, and although I heard him muttering to the grapefruits, he ate a grapefruit for breakfast and a grapefruit for dinner the whole week. I saw him slip one into his backpack in a brown paper bag as a sort of packed lunch.

"You can't live on grapefruit alone," I told him.

"I'm worried about scurvy," he said.

Sketch's girlfriend, Meg, did have naked pictures on the internet. Sketch had mass emailed them out with the subject line: "Check out my new girl" along with several winking emojis. The story was modern and romantic. He had seen her pictures, liked them, and the two of them had formed a tenuous friendship, primarily based on explicit text messages and suggestive phone calls. Eventually they had met in person, hit it off, and now they were official.

"Well, I'm not going to do better than this," Sketch said in another email. Alex showed me the correspondence. He was unable to conceive that some conversations were private and some were public. Everything was a matter of public record. He had been crashing on my couch for two weeks, and the endless chatter was starting to get on my nerves.

We were supposed to be meeting Sketch and the girlfriend at Tim Kellerman's bar for a quasi-double date, except Alex and I weren't a couple and Sketch's girlfriend got naked on camera.

"How can I talk to her?" Alex said during the car ride over. His hand was trembling slightly as he smoked his cigarette. "I've seen her boobs."

"Sketch has seen her boobs, and he talks to her."

"That's different."

I tried to remember the last time Alex had had a girlfriend. Or a boyfriend. Or anyone. He blew smoke out of his nostrils. "If I start being an idiot, kick me or something, okay?"

I reached my foot across the floor of the car and kicked him, softly, on the ankle bone.

"Point taken." He gave me a lopsided smile.

Tim Kellerman's bar was not owned by Tim Kellerman, but the name had stuck somehow. It was a horrible place, but it was five minutes from my apartment, and a PBR and a shot were four bucks every day but Saturday. We were there so much the bartenders knew us by name.

Alex got picky at bars. I hoped that the familiarity of Tim Kellerman's would alleviate the uneasiness that seemed to be coming out of him in waves.

Sketch and Alex had been better friends once, but Sketch had grown up. Alex was a burnout who collected fruit and worked two days a week.

Sketch was a drink and a half ahead of us when we sat down, a pitcher of beer half-empty in front of him. Meg had a sweet, open face and a pink cocktail in front of her. They made a strange couple. Sketch was large, square, and bulking, and Meg was tiny and smiley. She stood up to kiss me on the cheek and hugged Alex, who shimmied away from her touch. I tried to smile back at her, but Alex had planted the seed in my head. All I could think about was the photos. I had difficulty making eye contact with her.

"The weather's been nice lately," she said. I thought about her naked.

"Heard we'll have some rain later in the week." I thought about her naked.

The bartender brought over another pitcher and two clean glasses. I dumped beer into my glass so I didn't have to look at her face. Alex waved the bartender down for a vodka soda but poured himself a beer while he waited. I watched him out of the corner of my eye as Meg tried valiantly to make conversation.

"Sketch told me that you work in food service," she said, looking for agreement. Sketch was sometimes capable of coherent sentences, but he remained silent, staring protectively at his beer.

"I'm a waitress, if that's what you mean."

A server appeared with Alex's drink. He threw back half of it in a single swig and set the glass down a little too hard.

"And, Alex, what do you do?" Her smile was placid and friendly. I felt bad for her. She seemed like a nice, normal girl.

Sketch snorted. He seemed drunk. "Alex doesn't *do* anything." Alex raised one eyebrow, a dark arch on his pale face. "Alex is a writer," Sketch clarified when it became apparent that Alex would offer no defense. He said "writer" like it was a dirty word.

"He's been doing some shifts at the bookstore downtown," I said, putting my hand over Alex's. Meg saw the gesture, but kept her mouth shut.

"Good for him," Sketch said. "It's still not a real job."

"What I do isn't a real job either."

"You actually do something," he said. "Standing around with musty old books for a few hours a week isn't a job."

"Alex has plans," I said, squeezing my fingers shut around Alex's. He swallowed the rest of his drink and signaled for another one. "Alex, tell Sketch what you want to be when you grow up."

Alex looked at him and shrugged his shoulders. "I don't know," he said. "Maybe a cowboy."

"What?" Sketch rolled up the sleeves of his work shirt so the tattoos on his arms were visible.

Alex sighed, as if this were common knowledge, as if he were explaining it to a very simple person. "In the 1980s," he said, "there was this thing called cattle tick fever. All the cows were dying. Because, you know, fever. So the U.S. started a quarantine so the cows would stop dying." He tapped a cigarette out of his pack but didn't light it. "So now there are all of these federally funded cowboys who run the Tex-Mex border making sure the Mexican cows don't accidentally infect the quarantined American ones." He grinned, a little too wide. "Isn't that neat?"

Alex's second drink was placed on the table. He drained his beer glass and then started in on the other drink. "What happens if they do?" Meg asked. "Like, accidentally infect our cows?"

"The cowboys snare the Mexican cow, and then they take it to a facility and dip it in a vat of chemicals. Then they auction it back to the Mexican government." Alex looked extremely pleased with himself. "So that's what I want to do, like, if I could choose."

"Wow," Meg said. "That's so cool." She smiled, genuinely. I wondered why a girl like this was bothering with Sketch.

Sketch made a fist. "That's the stupidest thing I've ever heard," he said. "What are you going to do with a cowboy? You're a white guy from Boston."

"I'm not going to do anything with a cowboy," Alex said. His cheeks were getting redder. "I'm going to be the cowboy." He said it like it was obvious. A mean smirk had appeared on his face. Sketch's knuckles were white now, and straining.

"All right," Sketch said, his fingers curling around his glass. "Listen. I was tired of your attitude when you were twenty-one and it was cute. You're an adult now, man. You're embarrassing yourself. It's time to grow up."

"Don't tell me what to do," Alex said in a slow, measured voice. He was provoking Sketch now, and I didn't know how much longer Sketch could hold it in. He had always been very tightly wound.

Meg looked like she wanted to make a break for the door. She caught my eye and reached pointedly for her pack of cigarettes.

"I'm not telling you what to do," Sketch said. "You're the one making the mistake, man."

I stood up. "Alex, maybe we should go out for some air."

Meg stood too. "That sounds like a good idea." She smiled uncomfortably. The image of her naked popped unhelpfully into my head again. "Sketch, maybe you'd like to go with me? I think I need something from the car."

He looked at her like she was a fly he had just swatted out of the air, incredulous that she could be talking to him. "There's nothing in the car," he said.

"I just want to check. I think I lost something," she said. He didn't take the hint.

"Anything you need, you can get when we go home." He drained his glass and poured himself another beer from the pitcher.

She looked at her phone. "You know, I have to work tomorrow. Maybe we should call it a night."

"Cats have a basal body temperature of 101.5 degrees," Alex added innocuously. He smiled at Sketch, who slammed his full glass down on the table. A fingerling crack lanced through the glass.

"That's it," he said, looking at me. "Tanya, get him out of my sight."

We left Sketch with the tab. I had to lead Alex to the car. He was a little drunk. His cheeks were as pink as his hair, which flopped indelicately into one eye.

"'M fine," he said, slurring slightly as we got into the car. "Just had a bit more than I thought is all."

"You're not fine," I said, positioning a plastic bag in front of him. I preferred that he not vomit in my car. The ride was short and silent, and I helped him up the stairs.

He made a beeline for the bathroom, stood in front of the sink for several minutes, staring in the mirror, and then walked to the bed, pulled off his T-shirt, and laid down. I watched as he struggled to kick off his shoes.

"That's my bed," I said, prodding him with my fist. "Dude, move. Go sleep on the couch."

"'S fine," he mumbled, pulling the blankets over his head.

"Okay, I'll go sleep on the couch." I kicked off my shoes and pulled my dress over my head. I wasn't looking forward to a night on the lumpy couch, but Alex was sprawled and unresponsive.

"Don't go," he said. "It's fine."

"Alex," I said.

"I don't wanna be alone tonight," he said, quiet. "I won't do anything. I'll be good. Just stay, okay? So I don't wake up in the middle of the night." He reached out and made a stumbling grab for my wrist. "Please, Tanya. You're my best friend."

I pulled a loose T-shirt over my head and sat down next to him. He was so drunk it looked like he was moving through liquid, his movements slow and viscous. "Thank you," he said. It sounded like a smear against the dark. He turned so he was on his back, and I laid down and stared at the ceiling. We lay there, not touching. Eventually I fell asleep.

The morning was cool and open. My head felt like it was splitting open, but I didn't move, just watched the sun come in through the blinds. It set a dappled pattern over everything. Alex was either asleep or pretending to be, rolled over on his side, hair flopped down in his face. I watched his ribcage rise and fall. I put my hand on his ribs, felt the bones underneath. I couldn't remember the last time we had been this close to one another.

"Mm," Alex said and pulled the blankets away from me. I kicked him lightly. He rolled toward me, his arm draping heavily over my side.

"Alex," I said. "Why do you have to be such a jerk to everyone?"

"It's just the way I'm built," he said.

We cut up a pineapple for breakfast. Its name was George. Alex chattered the whole time. He was full of energy.

"Isn't it a bit like cannibalism, eating the fruit you've named?" I was not full of energy. I was face deep in a large mug of coffee, trying to choke down the chunks of pineapple, while Alex fried eggs in a pan. "Why do you name them anyway?"

"I like fruit," he said. "They're meant to be eaten. It would be meaner if I didn't eat them, you know?" He gave me a sweet, wide smile. "You just have to honor them is all. You can't just be cutting fruit up left and right. You have to be responsible about it." He looked away wistfully, and I knew he was thinking about the watermelon.

I tried to imagine Alex in a corporate job, or even waiting tables, bartending, something where he would have to get up at the same time every day and do the same thing. I tried to imagine him with hair a normal color, wearing clothes that weren't lime green or full of holes or held together by duct tape. I tried to imagine a world where he didn't bring home fruit or talk about ocelots or collect nonsense.

"Alex," I said. "What do you want?"

He looked at me, his nose wrinkling. "I want to be happy," he said.

The Right One

IT WASN'T THAT she didn't like him. Together they had a fast, loose, hurried intimacy that she rather liked, a kind of rapport that led to hands grabbing and other motions during the car ride home, not to mention what happened in the elevator and on the couch and in bed. He was Greek, in his forties, play-acting as a younger man with his silly Hawaiian shirts and his trip-hop music. She was twenty-six, in Athens on a vacation that had turned into an over-stay on her visa, in love with the raucous Greek who she heard in the stairwell of the building in which she lived, the food that seemed both endless and confusing for her, the American, and nightclubs unlike those she had seen in New York. No, Athens was not like New York.

Perhaps this is why she had stayed. It wasn't for him, him and the girlfriend whose shadowy presence had dominated the three months of their relationship. The girlfriend was in Lithuania caring for her sick father, and Nico didn't know when she would be back. Leah could hear him some nights, silently padding out of the bedroom when he thought she was asleep, then on the phone, whispering to her. He never said her name aloud.

Nico was one of many men Leah would know in her life. He was not the reason she was staying, but was part of it, she had to admit, and it wasn't that she didn't like him.

She couldn't put her finger on it. She had been in love before—a college boyfriend, who she had thought she would marry. When that didn't work out, there had been a procession of incongruous and inappropriate others. Nico was one of these. She was searching, scouring, she could feel it—but for what? She couldn't put her finger on it.

The passion between her and Nico, the blasts of laughter, the way he flirted openly with other women in front of her, it frightened her. She didn't want to feel so strongly, not after such a short period of time, not in such a foreign place. It wasn't that they were mismatched, because of course they were. Their relationship had a timestamp, and the clock was ticking.

"Don't think so much," Nico told her often, when he saw the lines appear in her forehead, the expression on her face taking on the pensive look of the great philosophers, those ironically Ancient Greeks. His accent serrated like the torn edges of expensive paper. "Baby, you're only hurting yourself."

Like most of the time, he was right. But Leah didn't want to admit that. She wanted to be the right one for once, the one with all the answers. Nico, his torso tight from crunches, his arms taut from the pull-ups he did on the bar above his door each morning—he had the body of a much younger man—he was just a hair short of instructional, bordering on condescending.

"Maybe I want to be hurt," she said the most recent time he had caught her too deep in her thoughts at a bar they both liked for its loud but not unbearable music and laid-back vibe. "Maybe you're the cat, and I'm the mouse. Maybe you like playing with me." She smiled coyly over the swizzle stick in her drink.

He smiled back, toothy as a shark. "Maybe it's this instead," he said. "Maybe you like being played with."

Nico ran a nightlife tour for tourists—the mostly English-speaking visitors to Greece who wanted a taste of the real Athens and were willing to pay a guide to accompany them through the winding, confusing, and sometimes sketchy nightlife district. Coming from Brooklyn six months prior, Leah had felt like she was familiar with the club scene there; she had spent many nights bouncing to techno at Mood Ring and Bossa Nova Civic Club, but this was something else.

As she accompanied him on these tours, and eventually became a tour guide herself, she learned about Athens' history and the way the clubs had evolved around these twisted, active roads. These lessons were ephemeral; later, when she tried to recall them, all she could ever recall were dizzy, spinning, drunken blurs of color and light. Drinkers and dancers hung out in the streets, moving to avoid passing cars, their glittering outfits briefly illuminated in the headlights. These nights were ripe with possibility, but they always ended up the same—with her and Nico drunk, stuporous, crash-landing into bed.

There was no *real* Athens, she had discovered—cities are what you make of them. But she was starting to feel at home as she worked her way through the unevenly paved streets. Nico would meet her at Mareka, a hole-in-the-wall with a head-pounding DJ and surprisingly delicious cocktails. She walked slowly, savoring the feeling of being alone in a strange city, hearing unfamiliar sounds, seeing unfamiliar sights, even as they had begun to seem commonplace in the six months she had been there. New York, where she had lived for eight years before coming to Athens, was nothing compared to this. No city was as alive as this, as bustling, as brilliant.

She was starting to put down roots. She was making friends. Maybe she would stay. She turned the idea over in her head as she walked, dodging to avoid a group of gesturing French tourists. Everyone has a place, she thought. Maybe this was hers. But did it include Nico?

Like a ghost, he emerged from behind a street sign. He was waiting for her. "Hi," he said, his voice giving nothing away, his subtle touch at her waist betraying nothing. Leah could never understand what he was feeling, thinking. It was one of the many parts of their relationship that frustrated her.

"Hey."

"How was your day?"

She began to answer, but his first client was already approaching, and Nico launched into work mode, his ultra-professional and super-friendly fake American accent. He had specifically instructed her that when he spoke like this, she was not to mention they were involved or act like they were a couple in public. "Sometimes, to get good reviews at this job, I have to flirt with customers," he had told her more than once. "It has nothing to do with you, and you can't take it personally."

This was a directive, not a suggestion. The business came first, leaving her to play second fiddle and try to entertain herself as he worked, vying for his attention as more beautiful and more interesting women passed in front of him, and she worked hard not to notice.

She made awkward small talk with the couple who had arrived from England and were joining them on the tour, and lit a cigarette for something to do with her hands. She had quit smoking, but in Europe, everyone smoked, and it was easy to pick up the habit again, like slipping into bed with an ex-lover. Leah hadn't meant to pick up smoking again, but it had happened anyway, somehow without her even deciding it, and like many aspects of her life, she felt like it was out of her control.

Alcohol would help heal the bruise to her ego. Tuning out Nico's voice, she ordered a drink at Mareka, which was behind them. On the tour, everyone got one free drink at the bar, but after three months at Nico's side, the bartender knew her and poured a heavy shot.

"Thanks, babe."

A curt nod and a five euro note in the tip jar. Americans were the only ones who tipped, but no one turned down the extra cash; it made bartenders like her, serve her more readily.

The liquor echoed its way down her throat. She felt its familiar pulse in her veins. Watching Nico talk to a dark-haired woman who had recently joined the group, she felt a surge of jealousy and motioned to the bartender for another.

It wasn't that she didn't like him. That much was clear to her now. Watching him with this woman—who was she, anyway? It made her blood boil. Rather, it was that she liked him too much. That she had what she wanted dangled in front of her, and she could not snatch it from the air the way a cat snatches a toy.

She made a sudden, sharp decision. If she could not handle these feelings, then she would feel nothing.

She ordered another shot.

Nico was a regular at a bar she frequented in her sub-letted neighborhood. They had met when he sat down at a table near hers, and in meet-cute fashion, he had asked her for a lighter.

"Sorry, I don't smoke," she said. This was before she had picked it up again, before she had begun her slow and steady decline into debauchery.

"I know," he said. "I was just looking for a reason to talk to you, but now you've made it obvious that my reason was bullshit."

They had talked for about an hour, inevitably gone back to his place. After that, he had seamlessly integrated her into his life, the way you fold a sheet and neatly put it away. She hung out at the bar with his friends, went on his tours, slept over at his apartment. He was very clear about the girlfriend, his open relationship, and his interest in non-monogamy. She wasn't looking for anything serious—at that point, she had been in Greece for only three months—and life felt fragile, tenuous, impermanent. Three months later, though, she felt as though he was the most tangible thing in her temporary, adopted life, the one constant that held everything together.

Of course, there were things she didn't like about him. But she was willing to sweep all of that away for that coveted happy ending. What wouldn't she give up? Her life in New York was a depressing nightmare. Copy editing at a men's magazine and paying an arm and a leg for a room in a shared apartment. Greece had been a dream. Who wouldn't want to stop dreaming when the dream looked like this?

Seven, eight drinks. Leah had stopped counting. Nico's hand on the small of her back, the cocaine they had shared in the bathroom. Thud of the bassline in her sternum. The girl she met on the dancefloor, their undulating bodies moving in perfect synchronization. Death; it will always be the mother of beauty. Across the room the DJ shone from his table like a beating heart, a fallen angel, an exploding star.

The English tourists had started making dirty jokes. Leah only wanted to dance, to move her body as if there were nothing else. She wanted oblivion, the purest possible hit of feeling, ego death. She could see out of the corner of her eye Nico whispering in a woman's ear, curving his mouth to fit into the shell of her neck, close as the click in a door. She tried not to look, but she looked, and she didn't like what she saw.

Nico had once told her that she would never belong to anyone. "Just be yourself," he said. "You are just enough. Be proud to be who you are. I've always respected you as an equal—you do know that, don't you?"

She glowed with pride. This older, successful man approved of her. He was owning her, in a way, branding her with his respect, and although she didn't yet know this, she would reference him for years when looking in the mirror or when thinking about how to conduct herself. He may have only been one in a procession of men, but the mark he made in the clay of her being was a deep one.

It was not love. She knew that, knew it in her bones, the way you know when someone is lying to you. It was something more sinister, more unique, and more terrifying. More complex than pure infatuation, it was an obsession between the two of them, a fascination with the kind of trinkets and tsotchkes you might find at a yard sale. She wanted both to kill and possess him. His respect—did she even want it? Could she possibly give it back? Return to sender. No, thank you, sir. I'll do without.

It wasn't that she didn't like him. No, she wished it could be that simple. It was that when they were together, he brought out her capacity for violence.

At their final destination. The tequila shot she swallowed, the closely packed dancers, the cigarettes exhaled and inhaled. Nico could tell something was wrong, and he was subtly attentive, touching her wrist, his face reddish and sweating in the muggy September Athens heat.

Time had ceased to exist. It was sometime before morning, and as long as the sun hadn't come up yet, it was all right to be awake. They were safe, solemn, sacred. Leah didn't know if she would ever sleep again.

"Do you need anything?" Nico offered her a cup of water, his hand grasping the sweating plastic. "Do you want another drink?"

"I'm okay."

Suddenly there was so much potential between them, potential for growth. She wanted to tell him how she felt but couldn't verbalize it. She wasn't even sure what she would say. To love someone is to own them, but also to relinquish yourself. Leah was pretty sure she didn't love Nico, but she was also pretty sure she didn't love herself.

One of the tourists who had been on the trip that night—a young fraternity-type Canadian boy—broke into their conversation. "I'm going to fuck someone tonight," he declared. Addressing Leah, he asked, "What are you up to?"

Nico flashed into defensive mode. "Excuse me, you can't speak to her like that. I need you to leave, now, or we're going to have a problem."

"What the fuck? I was just kidding."

A chill had run through Leah's body, and now she felt sick to her stomach. She felt her feet react before her head could catch up, and she was standing and walking out of the bar before Nico could say anything more. She avoided the frat guy and was dialing her home address into Uber when he found her outside.

The night was shockingly dark and quiet. "Leah. Hey. I'm sorry about that guy. Are you okay? Do you want me to take you home?"

"I'm fine. I'm just going to go."

"Let me take you back."

Leah imagined a night ride on the back of Nico's Vespa and felt even more ill. "It's okay. I'll just call a car."

"Please."

Dropping her phone into her purse, she numbly let him lead her to where he was parked. On the street, a few random drunks wobbled like zombies from spot to spot, shouting in unintelligible, spillover Greek. Nico ignored this and let Leah climb aboard the Vespa. She was crying, she realized—she hadn't even felt the wetness on her cheeks.

The wind whipped through her hair. My Greek adventure is over, she thought to herself as she took in the sights around her—neon slur, uneven cobblestones, weaving Vespa, Acropolis looming over it all. It's all over.

It wasn't about being right or wrong. It wasn't cat and mouse, endlessly chasing and catching and chasing again. She could hurt and be hurt, and she was. More than that, she was tired—tired of being treated like a child, of being condescended to, of looking for approval in all the wrong places.

She was learning. God help her, she was. Bit by bit, piece by piece. Each choice she made, it brought her closer to what she was looking for. As a child, she had meticulously recorded the names of the birds that had visited the bird feeder that had hung outside of her bedroom window. To see something is to name something is to believe in it. What was she seeing, what was she naming, and what did she believe? Like the birds at the feeder, she wanted to flit from moment to moment, but she was not that kind of person. She was horribly stuck in this instant. She simply could not take flight. Was this what they meant by *growing up?*

Uppers and Downers

WHEN I FIRST meet Dean, former bartender and regular at the bar on the corner of the block I live on in Bushwick, he comments that I drag on my cigarettes so the smoke goes all the way into my lungs, rather than just letting it stay in my mouth, and I tell him the truth, which is that I learned to smoke cigarettes from being around hardcore weed smokers. Each day they sat in huge circles and passed joints around until they got so high they floated up into the air like balloons, and if they hadn't tied themselves to something, it was hard to predict where they would land when the high wore off; this could be potentially dangerous. In health class in ninth grade, Mr. Gagstetter made sure to mention that if we intended to smoke weed, please don't do it on school property (we all joked that he was just trying to avoid liability), and please, please, anchor yourself, tie or attach yourself.

Even with his warning, more than one freshman landed in the East River that semester, and they became laughingstocks, basically forever.

Weed wasn't really my thing. I didn't like the weird twist it put on everything, the detached and distanced echo it added to the world. I was confused enough as it was without adding another layer of complexity. Some kids got into pills, that was the rumor, but no one ever left the school in a scandal kind of way except for two girls.

The first one was someone I knew well. Zola was one of the first friends I made, and she showed me all kinds of interesting things. On one of the first days of school, we went to St. Marks, and she got a tattoo from a dude in one of the booths. The tattoo looked like shit, but it was like $60, and she was only fourteen; it wasn't her first tattoo either. At her urging, I got an industrial ear piercing. It was $20. I didn't need ID, and I didn't need to sign anything. Over the next few months, I got a number of ear piercings and also a belly button piercing. This friend of mine, she made me feel brave. This was high school; I was on my way to independence. My mother's reaction, which wasn't great, didn't matter because it was already done, and she couldn't really do anything about it. She just made me promise to keep the metal out of my face, if I could, and I respected that for the entirety of my teens.

Those first few weeks of high school were full of excitement at our new freedom. Zola and I went to the movies with Russell, another student in our class. It was clear that Russell had wanted a date, and Zola had warded him off by inviting me. But he was enthusiastic, and we ended up having a great time.

I didn't realize at first, but with Zola, it wasn't weed, it was everything. And the teachers knew, everyone knew. It wasn't the kind of thing you could hide. Once she took some pills and showed up to school with no arms, although they grew back when she waited a while. Once she was covered in black fur. Once she could only speak German. It was often funny, and at times I wished I was having these experiences with her, but most of the time it was disruptive, although I didn't mind because it was better than the monotony of high school. The teachers, however, immediately sounded the alarm. She was hustled into the principal's office and threatened with expulsion if she didn't start giving up names. Her home life wasn't great, and I knew the chaos she would suffer if she was kicked out of school. She gave names, a few names. And it spiraled, and then it spiraled some more.

My best friend, Charlie, was a hard drug user, or at least that's what he told me. This was quite a bit after the situation with Zola, but I hadn't met Charlie yet when that had gone down. In high school there weren't a lot of people doing heavy drugs like that because the academics were demanding, and if people were taking stimulants, they were taking Adderall so they could keep up with their coursework. Something like cocaine wasn't easy to get as a teenager, and even if they could get it, it was expensive, and most teens don't have access to that much money on a regular basis. Charlie fell into it after taking on someone else's debt when his friend was unexpectedly caught by his parents and sent to wilderness rehab; my guess is he started taking it to keep up with the stress of managing the drug dealing and the pressures of school, particularly because he took a gap year between high school and college. He wasn't ready, and I'm one of the few people who know why.

It took him a while before he told me. I had noticed the snakes, of course, that were winding around his wrists. And his shadow was gone, even when the day was sunny. Sometimes when I asked him a question, he gave me a string of numbers instead of words. This wasn't immediately referential to drug abuse though—sometimes when people were stressed, this kind of thing could happen. It hadn't happened to me, but my mother had told me about it, and she said I shouldn't worry too much if it started to happen to me because it was just a regular part of life.

No one knew about Charlie's drug use, not really. He was careful about that, hiding the snakes as best he could. But people gossip. We were all gossiping about Anya, for example, dating Lucas. This was the second of the two scandals. Lucas was the drug dealer who took over when Charlie graduated; this was how it always worked: A rising junior made a deal with the graduating senior, and the senior introduced this person to their connect. Anya was gorgeous, one of the most beautiful girls I've ever seen, and Lucas was made of a gelatinous substance, without bones and slightly transparent, oozing from place to place. To accommodate this, the school provided containers in his classrooms so he could focus on his schoolwork, rather than straining to maintain a more solid corporal form. Anya didn't seem to mind the bonelessness. Lucas was the kingpin that particular year, and Anya had a drug problem, so they were the natural pair.

Their prom photos are sweet, they look so happy. But Anya went to rehab for cocaine and came back addicted to heroin. From social media now, as I stalk her pages years later, it seems she has finally gotten clean, but she and Lucas are no longer a couple. I don't know what happened to Lucas, and I don't know what happened to Charlie either.

The most popular girl in our grade is Instagram famous now, which tracks. She was confident and outspoken, and she has good hair.

She was one of the names on Zola's list, and the administration questioned her, but like everyone else they spoke to, nothing really came of it. They started being more conscious of those circles out in the yard. And of course there were the sinkholes.

Some of these kids probably had legitimate prescriptions, but there was an issue with benzos—mostly Klonopin—which affected a number of students, in particular those who were also abusing Adderall to study more effectively. The two drugs used in tandem helped students to come up or down in a controlled manner based on what they needed in that moment. If they had a few spare hours, a K-pin could help them sleep, and if they needed to pull an all-nighter, they could pop an Addy and keep going with no breaks until everything was done.

The Klonopin, however, had the unfortunate effect of pulling students down and into the floor. As they drifted off to sleep with their heads on their desks, they started to sink down, through the linoleum and then into the floor itself. In a few cases, students who had misjudged dosages had actually fallen through the ceiling and into the classroom directly below, causing all kinds of chaos and very expensive repairs to the building because the damage threatened the structural integrity of the classrooms affected. Moving the classes and finding space for the students to work became top priority, right after they continued to grill Zola for information, hoping she was the key to make these events stop. Zola went silent, and they threatened to kick her out again, and, well, you get the idea.

While Zola sweated it out in the principal's office, Russell and I were conspiring. We didn't want to see her expelled, but we knew she was in trouble, and we didn't know why.

"Her dad sucks," I told him. "She told me he just sits on the couch and doesn't do anything. But he collects disability, and he gives her money."

"I wish she didn't have to live with him," Russell said. "I wish we could adopt her."

I was dubious of Russell's affection, because even though I loved Zola, she was very complicated and often, obscure. She was always making cryptic references, and most of the time I didn't feel like I was in on the joke. Zola was my friend, but I didn't really get how someone would want to be with her in that way, but maybe, I told myself, I was just being judgmental.

Zola was confident even though she wasn't pretty, and she wasn't really even that smart. She was manipulative, and she knew how to talk people into doing what she wanted. She was a good salesperson, and she was comfortable with herself. Whenever we went anywhere together, people usually wanted to talk to me instead of her because I was more conventionally attractive, but I was shy and awkward and not comfortable with the beauty that I would settle into when I was older and had more awareness and control. Zola didn't care what people thought, if they thought she was pretty or smart or interesting. She was fearless, and she would do anything. You didn't even have to give her anything in return; she did things just to do them. She just wanted to see what would happen. She wanted to push every boundary, the way a cat knocks a glass off a table just to watch it shatter.

This would be a running theme—doubt from all sides. When Dean began dating Ramona, I was annoyed because of how similar we are. He turned me down and chose her. Ramona and I are built on the same mold, and I can see he has a type, but I'm peeved by this particular revelation, even though I really like Ramona and I'm glad they're happy—they both deserve it—and I think they're a good match. They are both incredibly caring, observant, and compassionate people. I can't stop myself from the knee-jerk reaction though, and I don't say anything, but for some reason it really bothers me.

It was the popular girl with good hair and lots of Instagram followers who started the whole bullying thing. Russell and I talked as we sat next to each other in our creative writing class, but the whole grade had turned against Zola, and we had to be quiet about our dissent.

"Everyone hates her," he said. "She didn't do anything."

"I think that's the point. We don't know what she did, so everyone is assuming the worst."

There was a Facebook group for our grade where students made announcements or asked for notes and homework from classes if they had been absent or hadn't written it down. Shiloh had made a post denigrating Zola, and it had gone up on all kinds of social media, where it was rapidly shared between members of our grade, and suddenly it was like a wildfire that couldn't be put out, and people were saying all kinds of mean things. I had texted Zola to see if she was okay, but she hadn't responded. She wasn't in our sixth-period Spanish, the only class we had together. I knew she hadn't been expelled, so I didn't know where she was. I felt helpless.

The popular girl with the good hair was flanked by a lot of support. There was the girl who had such a perfect body that even in a crop top and leggings, her tail was almost invisible. Another girl frequently climbed the walls with the sticky pads of her hands, like a gecko. No one smoked cigarettes because they were bad for you, but everyone vaped; they took the toilets out of the girls bathrooms on the third floor so anyone who wanted to vape in private had a safe space, as it still wasn't allowed in the classrooms. You didn't need a pass; if you were in class and you needed to go, as long as you were quiet and didn't disturb other students, it wasn't a problem. The school prided itself on the concept that if you treat teenagers like adults, they will rise to the occasion.

The bullying that Zola was experiencing, however, was beyond the regular scope of teenage mischief. She was pushed around in the halls, and then her shoelaces were tied together. Someone took a video as she stumbled around trying to fix this, and it was sent all around the school. Someone made a reaction video and wrote an original song using a Kendrick Lamar sample, and for a week or two the song was sung, quietly, under someone's breath all over the school—you couldn't go ten feet without hearing it in the background like an echo or the hum of static.

The teachers and the staff must have known, but they didn't say anything, and they didn't do anything. I think they were hoping to isolate her, place her under stress, so she would give up more information. Zola was becoming her own kind of pressure cooker, and she wasn't just being egged on by the students. The teachers and the administration, everyone was in on it. As Joseph Heller wrote, "Just because you're paranoid doesn't mean they're not after you."

"People just keep adding and adding and making it worse." Russell paused after watching this all go down. "Do you have her address? We could go to her house."

I shook my head. I didn't have it. I knew vaguely what direction it was in, way on the west side of Manhattan, but I wasn't even sure what street. There was no way we could find her. "I guess we just have to see what happens."

Russell felt helpless too. I could see it in his face. The carrots embedded in his forehead had been almost ready to be picked, but now the previously green tops were curling and turning yellow as he worried about our friend.

The night that I think of as the turning point with Dean is the one that I remember and he doesn't. I won't repeat the more explicit details. There were comments made on both sides that were inappropriate. Dean always said he was too old for me; I was twenty-four, and he was forty-two. I wished for less of a gap. I was mature for my age, and he admitted that. I was smoking my cigarette in the way that I did when I wanted to draw attention to my mouth, my red lipstick. He was hesitating, but I knew how to push forward; men are frighteningly simple in some ways and totally confounding in others.

We've always flirted, Dean and I. And we both like to push the limits. But that night he went too far. And it opened a door that shouldn't have been opened. I asked him about it later, and he claimed not to remember; he was too drunk. I believe it, I choose to believe it, because it's true—he was very drunk. But I heard it, and I know what happened. I saw the fish scales that appeared like magic scrolls glittering on his hands as they gripped mine.

It was a while before I pushed my own limits with him and tried to see how far I could go. This time it was him who turned me down. Although we had always played games, this was the real thing. We both agreed to tone it down. But when he shoved into the bar with all his drunken bluster and I detached myself from his too tight hug, telling him I wouldn't be led on, I wouldn't let him offer me something I couldn't actually have, I was surprised when I saw the flash of jealousy as I kissed someone else, later in the night. I won't have the object I covet shoved in my face and then snatched away, the way a toddler plays with a toy or a cat with a mouse. I won't be embarrassed by my own instincts. I want a sure thing. I won't show my cards again in this lifetime. Why is it that we always want what we can't have? Why is it that we can't just accept what we have and agree that it's enough?

*

It's months, and we don't hear it from Zola herself. Somehow it worked through the grapevine that she was in some kind of hospital or psych ward because of the bullying. She was safe and she was alive and she was doing better, but yes, she had tried to kill herself.

I wanted to be surprised when the news washed over me, but I wasn't. By this point I was changing too; my eyes were two different colors, one brown and one yellow. I could turn my head 270 degrees, like an owl. I had wings, but I hadn't told anyone. That was just for me.

The same questions kept coming up. With any suicide, attempted or completed, the question is always *why?* She was under a lot of pressure, and she wasn't doing well academically. Socially she wasn't doing well either. Russell and I were her only friends. Everyone thought she ratted on them, and there was no way anyone was going to forgive her. It was ninth grade, and she would have gone through three more years of abuse. Of course, this is not a reason to attempt suicide, but I understand, in a way, that she felt trapped, out of options, unable to find support from authority figures, with only one way out.

I've been there, the knife in your hand, the blood in the sink. The pill bottle beckons you to shake more than your prescribed allotment. I have had those dreams, and I know the release seems so quiet and safe. But the only reaction to this kind of action is destruction. I know this now, and I can never unknow it.

It was clear that she would not be returning to our school. By that point Charlie and I were best friends. Russell started dating someone, and we remained friends, but his girlfriend was threatened by me, and he and I became more and more distant. Why didn't I do anything? Why didn't either of us say anything? I just kept moving forward. After high school was over, I did my best not to look back.

I admit that I was strung out when I saw Zola on the C train. The A was running with delays, and I was trying to get home so I could take out cash and text my dealer. The irony of it all is that after witnessing the damage that drugs can do, I had ended up just as addicted as everyone else. I was tired from working all day at the graphic design firm where I was a junior designer. I wanted to pick up, go get a beer, and chill out for a few hours, a little bit of a break from the constant barrage of items on my to-do list.

Zola waved at me. We'd spoken on Facebook Messenger a few times over the years, but quite honestly I couldn't remember a single detail of her life. After she changed schools, we lost touch. Russell, on the other hand, I ended up staying friends with, kind of. We didn't speak until he came back to New York after college, but since he's been back in the last few years, we've made a point of hanging out every once in a while. There weren't many people from high school I was still in touch with, so it was nice in a way to have that.

I gave her a stilted hello because my head was pounding. She blurted before I could speak: "How have you been?"

I gave her the rundown: communications design at Pratt, some very stressful months freelancing, a paid internship at a small design firm that led to a recommendation that led to my current junior position, which paid okay and provided really shitty health insurance. I wasn't dating at the moment. "I'm just trying to focus on getting more connected to what I actually want."

The truth was that when Charlie stopped speaking to me, I lost the ability to trust what people tell me. Vulnerability was out of the question. I could no longer believe anyone when they made promises or tried to commit to me, and it had ruined every relationship I had ever been in.

"Wow, that's great!" She seemed genuinely enthusiastic, and she looked good, healthy, color in her face, not too thin and not too heavy. "I've been trying to figure it all out. I'm working in a bookstore, but I'm not sure what I want to do, like, for a career. Or even if I want that."

"Yeah, I get that." I considered getting off a stop early and walking an extra ten minutes so I didn't have to talk to her for a long time. "It's hard to figure out what you're actually most fulfilled by."

"Right, exactly." She laughed. "You were always the one who knew it all."

"Uh, right."

"No, I mean it."

I let out a laugh that felt forced. "Well, that's a nice thing to say."

"We should hang out!" She was so excited that I wondered for a second—maybe she was just really lonely. "Do you live around here?" She gestured to the C train, which had just stopped at Clinton-Washington. I thought about lying. "I'm on Franklin."

Shit, she was close. We could run into each other accidentally. "Yeah, I'm a little bit farther out."

"You still have my number?"

Because I couldn't get out of it, I dug through my contacts and confirmed she had the same number and texted it so she had my number, then made a note to be mysteriously busy at any time she suggested we get together. Franklin came up, and she threw her body toward mine in an awkward hug. "So glad to see you!" she chirped. "It was totally fate. We were destined to be friends again."

This persona was so different from the fearless and surly teenager I had known, and I wondered if she had been swapped out with a robot of some kind, but this was an ungenerous thought, and I quickly dismissed it. I gave her another wave as she drifted onto the platform. I knew that I had wings now, big wings, lots of feathers, and I could fly very high, but I didn't have to prove anything to anyone, and I certainly didn't have to prove anything to her. I didn't have to hide the snakes around my own wrists. The sky was the limit. I went home and I changed my clothes and I bought drugs and I went to the bar and I got blackout drunk alone and avoided people who tried to speak to me, sometimes rudely, because people don't change even if it seems like they do, they don't.

Emergency Contact

THE CALL CAME in around four in the afternoon. Teddy hadn't been doing anything, but he hadn't expected anything to disrupt him either. He had been unemployed for two months. Before that, he had been a graphic designer at a relatively well-known magazine. There had been layoffs. He hadn't been looking for a new job, enjoying living off of unemployment checks and having leisure time for the first time in his adult life, which had been colored by student loans and hard work. "A guy could get used to this," he told his girlfriend, Elizabeth, over dinner one night. She disapproved of his new lifestyle. He had gained weight from drinking beer in the middle of the day, and often she came home from her fast-paced job as a lawyer for a midsize corporation to find him napping on the couch. But none of that mattered once he got the call.

"Your wife has been in a car accident," the voice on the other end said, succinct and matter-of-fact.

"I don't have a wife," Teddy said. He didn't.

"You're not married to Rosemary Owens, 318 Himrod Street, Brooklyn, New York, 11237?"

"Not anymore," Teddy said. "Not for two years now."

"Either way," the voice said. "You're her emergency contact. She's at Beth Israel Hospital."

The voice hung up.

"I want you to keep an open mind," Julian said. Julian and Teddy had gone to art school together. They had looked for jobs together and ended up being roommates. Through their midtwenties, they had mostly partied. Teddy had bartended and done some freelance work and eventually gotten a full-time graphic design job, and then a studio apartment, but Julian had family money and intended to sleep with every model in Manhattan who he could convince that he had "industry connects" and could introduce them to major photographers, which he was pretty persuasive about and fairly believable until you checked his Instagram account and saw he followed more than two thousand accounts but had only 231 followers. That was usually around the time girls smiled and said they would be right back but they had to use the restroom, and later he would pass them in another part of the bar, talking to someone else. Teddy was twenty-nine, and he felt like maybe it was time to stop fucking around, and Julian said he knew the perfect girl. Teddy was dubious, but the girl Julian had introduced him to was Rosemary. She was a few years younger and in teacher's college; she was the cousin of a girl Julian had been DM'ing, and she was interested in art, but her family was already at a loss about her older sister who was trying to be a model, so she was trying to be responsible. Julian said he had met her at a party, and she seemed like what Teddy was looking for. The girl Julian was dating was trying to make her cousin feel comfortable in the city because she seemed like she wasn't adjusting well, she hadn't made many friends. She didn't drink much, didn't party, she was smart and pretty, and Teddy knew he would marry her after about twenty minutes in the restaurant while they waited for the server to take their orders. He didn't bother to try to impress her; he was himself. He didn't want to lie to this girl. She was too special. When the real thing happens, you have to give it all you've got.

Teddy sat up from where he was lying on the couch. Rosemary had been in an accident. He tried to think of the last time he had seen her. Not since the lawyer's office when they had signed the papers officially separating from each other. There had been much vitriol between them at the end. A lot of screaming "I never want to see you again," and "My mother never liked you anyhow." A lot of tearing out his hair at the temples, which was only just beginning to regrow. He hadn't tried to see her after that. He had thought about it a hundred times, trying to mend fences, but he hadn't done it. And now he was still her emergency contact? In two years, she hadn't met someone else who she could call in times of crisis? What about her mother? No, she hated her mother. A friend? Rosemary didn't have many friends, at least not friends she could trust in a crisis. No, it had always been him she turned to in times of stress, and apparently, it still was.

He found himself getting off the couch, walking to the bedroom, pulling jeans out of a drawer, stripping off his day-old sweatpants, running a brush through his sticking-up hair. It didn't matter how he looked, he supposed; she was in the hospital. She wouldn't be judging him. But for some reason he wanted to look put together for her.

He imagined the accident as he looked for his keys. Smashed glass, screaming. He and Rosemary had been in a slight fender bender once, when they were still married. Insurance had paid out in full, and they went on vacation with the money. That was when things were still good between them, before he had slept with his coworker Tasha, and Rosemary decided he was a bastard. He had slept with Tasha only because things with Rosemary had gotten so bad. He didn't regret it. The sex had been average, but the way Tasha looked up to him (she had been twenty-two, he had been over forty) had made him feel so special that it was worth it. Rosemary never treated him like that.

There were a lot of things he missed about Rosemary. Her French toast in the mornings, for one. The way she smelled. The way she read books, with her thumb in her mouth, concentrating. The way she talked about the kids in her kindergarten class and sometimes did impressions, surprisingly good ones, imitating the five-year-olds and their ridiculous antics. She always had a funny story. "One of my kids pulled a loose tooth out of his mouth and threw it at another kid," she told him once. Or "One of the little girls climbed on another girl and onto the top of a bookshelf while the student teacher was in charge so I could go to the bathroom because I had just gotten my period and was bleeding through my pants. When I got back, the girl was on top of the bookshelf, and we couldn't get her down. The principal had to stand on a chair, and we basically had to drag her down." For a long time it had been good, really good. Then he had fucked it all up, or maybe they had both fucked it all up.

You couldn't lie to Rosemary. It was impossible. Julian had warned Teddy of this, but he was so taken by her that he had somehow convinced himself that this wouldn't be a problem, it would never be a problem. She had tried to explain it to him on the first date, and he was fine with it; he was an honest person, he would never lie, of course. She always knew, she said. It was a smell sometimes, or else it was a kind of aura, a sheen that people took on, or sometimes it was a warm feeling. It was different for everyone. Teddy kind of didn't believe it, but when they had been dating for a few months, she had asked him if he preferred one dress to another, and he had said something offhand, and she had gotten upset, and he realized that inadvertently, he had lied. He was anxious to leave the house because they were going to a holiday party at his job, and they were already late. He apologized, and it was fine, but that should have been the moment when he walked away. He didn't walk away, and they were married for fourteen years. Julian had warned him. His new girlfriend, Elizabeth, he had met on a dating site. She was a journalist, and she was straightforward and easygoing. Rosemary could be very high strung and, at times, vindictive. Elizabeth was calmer and more stable. It was a relief in a lot of ways after walking on eggshells for so long, picking his words so carefully. But that didn't mean he didn't love her, or had loved her; it didn't mean he hadn't given fourteen years of his life to her; and it didn't mean he didn't care.

He tried to shake himself out of these thoughts as he walked out of the apartment, locking the door behind him.

He sent a quick text to Elizabeth that he wouldn't be home for dinner. He couldn't dwell on the past, he told himself. The past was the past. He needed to stay in the present moment. He needed to think about Rosemary—her well-being, her future. If she listed him as her emergency contact, obviously she still needed something from him; support, empathy, kindness, and he was going to try his best to provide, no matter what it took.

Teddy had forgotten his deep love of hospitals. As a lifelong hypochondriac, they made him feel safe—all those doctors and nurses, bustling back and forth. The hospital was like a gigantic organism, whirring away, safe and clean. He followed the stream of people up to the third floor, where the ICU was, and he asked around until he was able to locate her room and her doctor, who was talking to another patient. He didn't want to go in and see her without talking to someone first, so he loafed around the waiting room for a few minutes, went to the cafeteria and got a cup of coffee, and came back to talk to Dr. Felsenfeld, a tanned and efficient man with a clipboard and two stethoscopes around his neck.

"Three-car pileup, taxi driver, very nasty," the doctor said, tapping his fingers on his clipboard. "She's lucky to be alive. Some bruised ribs, some internal bleeding. We got her into surgery and repaired most of the damage, but now it's just a question of when she'll wake up. She got a pretty good knock on the head there."

"A concussion then?" Teddy wracked his brains for every bit of medical knowledge he had gleaned from watching *Grey's Anatomy.*

"A concussion, yes. The CT scan shows no bleeding in the brain, so she's going to be okay. She'll be groggy from the anesthesia, but she'll be fine in a few hours if you want to go sit with her."

"She's not my wife," Teddy explained. "She's my ex-wife. I only came because she listed me as her emergency contact on some form somewhere."

"I see," the doctor said with the practiced air of someone who truly did not care that much.

"I mean, I don't know if she wants me to be there when she wakes up," Teddy said.

"In my experience," the doctor said, "it's better to have someone there than no one at all. Stay a while. Maybe you'll learn something you didn't know."

"If you say so," Teddy said. But already he was thinking of French toast. He was thinking of Rosemary's smell.

Teddy had not meant to get divorced. He thought about this as he sat in Rosemary's hospital room, listening to the machines beep and ping. He had not meant to sleep with twenty-two-year-old Tasha, the intern, but they had gone out for drinks, and he had had one too many and fallen into bed with her almost too easily, as if it had been premeditated, as if it was always going to happen. He and Rosemary had been fighting. She wanted to have a baby. He did not. He would have acquiesced eventually; he knew this about himself now, at forty-five, discussing a last-ditch attempt at children with his girlfriend, Elizabeth. But at forty-two, he hadn't been convinced. He liked his life as it was—breakfast in bed, late nights at the office, the occasional drunken sex on the coffee table after happy hour drinks down at the bar they liked to go to on Wednesday afternoons when Rosemary got off work early. He had made it into his forties without a kid, and she was thirty-nine, and the chances just didn't seem likely at that point. If they were going to do it, they should have done it already. They had missed their window. She was always saying that it was possible now, women did it, they could keep trying or do IVF or go to a fertility doctor. She actually did go to a doctor at one point. She had her IUD removed, and he wore condoms for a while, but she asked him to stop, and he did. He was letting nature take its course, but he didn't expect a miracle.

So they fought, and he slept with intern Tasha, and he told Rosemary, but really he didn't have to, because she always knew, she knew everything, and she said, "I'm done," and went to stay with her sister in Astoria, and a few months later he was signing divorce papers.

He had taken his marriage vows seriously. Perhaps too seriously. He had assumed they would be able to get through anything. He had thought she would forgive. It was a massive miscalculation. She had been quiet at first, and then she had gone into the bedroom and begun packing. He wouldn't have done it, wouldn't have even thought of doing it, if she hadn't been hounding him about babies.

He said that. That made it even worse. "So it's my fault then?" she spat at him, throwing clothes into a duffel bag.

"I never said that," he said. "That's not what I'm saying at all. I'm just saying, we've been under a lot of stress lately."

"I'm done," she said, so quiet and sure it was almost a mantra. "I'm done, I'm done, I'm done."

Later he had wondered if she had secretly thought this for weeks and had just been waiting for him to mess up so she could leave without guilt. These were ugly thoughts, the kind of thoughts that only came to him late at night when he'd been drinking. Was their marriage always doomed? he wondered. Or was it really his fault? He never knew for sure. That didn't stop him from blaming himself. He oscillated between blaming himself and blaming her.

Looking at her face for the first time in two years, in the hospital bed, he realized he still blamed her for a lot of things. She had been cruel in the divorce proceedings, extracting every bit of money she could from him, even though he hadn't had much to begin with. Some stocks and bonds, some inheritance money. It had all gone to her. He remembered her sneer, her lawyer's sneer, the click of her high heels as she walked down the hall away from him for the last time.

There were bruises up and down the left side of her face, but she was still the same Rosemary she had always been—sharp and beautiful. She was growing her normally short hair out from the bob it had always been in since he'd known her. He wondered what else was different about her.

Suddenly the machines beeped louder, and he startled. She was opening her eyes. He didn't know how long he'd been sitting there—the clock read past midnight. Had he really been at the hospital that long? He should have called Elizabeth, he thought to himself. But instead he moved toward Rosemary.

"Hey," he said, unsure of what she would say when she saw his face. "How are you feeling?"

"Like I got hit by a car," she said. "Jesus."

"See, you don't understand why that's funny," he said. "But that's funny."

"No, I remember," she said. "Fuck. Can you get me some water?"

"Water? Sure."

He went to the adjoining bathroom with a plastic cup he found on the bedside table and filled it. She couldn't sit up due to the bruised ribs, but she could sip the water slowly through a straw.

"New York taxi drivers, huh?" Teddy said, trying to make conversation. "They'll kill ya."

"Last time I ever take a yellow cab," Rosemary said. "Look, I'm sorry to drag you down here. You don't have to stay. I don't need you here."

It seemed to pain her a lot to speak. He stayed quiet for a while, letting her drink her water. A nurse came in and took her vitals, said some things he didn't understand completely, and left.

"I'll stay," he said. "If you don't have anyone else to call."

"I have other people to call," Rosemary said defensively. She winced from the pain; the movement and intensity of her statement had been too sudden. "They called you because I haven't updated my insurance forms yet, I guess."

"From two years ago?" It seemed dubious.

"You know how I am with forms," she said. "I can't tell a W2 from my elbow."

That was true. When they were married, he had always been the one to deal with insurance, taxes, anything that involved filling out forms and anything official or dealing with the government. She was useless at it; she got frustrated and ended up making careless mistakes.

"So I'm not still your emergency contact on purpose?" he said.

"Of course not. We're not married anymore."

"I know that," he said. "Trust me, I know. Anyway," he started, "it's good to see you."

"You don't have to do that."

"Do what?'

"Pretend to be happy to see me."

"I'm not pretending."

"I know you have better things to do than sit in this hospital room with me. Don't you have some fancy party to go to or drinks or whatever?"

When they were married, she had always ribbed him that he was the more social of the two. He had liked to be out and about every night, always going to some party or art opening or event, and she had preferred to stay home or simply go out to their local bar where the bartenders knew their names. Evidently, she had not forgotten this.

"I have nothing else to do but stay with you until you feel better," Teddy said. "It's not like I can just turn off caring about you like you would turn off a switch."

"It's been two years." She wasn't accusing him of lying. It was more that her own emotions were overtaking his. Or that she was still angry. It was possible that the physical pain of the accident was amplifying her feelings. It was also possible that she just really hated him. He thought about the phone calls, right at the end. All of the calls he had ignored, the texts and the voicemails, and suddenly he wanted to throw up.

"I know how long it's been."

"You haven't moved on?" Her tone was accusatory. "You haven't just moved on and had some kind of perfect little life? Without me and my hospital visits?"

The guilt was welling up like blood in a cut. It was a mistake to come, to even think that she had wanted him to. But he wasn't going to be bullied so easily. "I have moved on, actually. I have a girlfriend. She's very nice. She's a journalist."

"So go home to her then. I'm fine." She wouldn't look at him either. The venom in her voice might have killed him on its own even without the emotions that were start-ing to pulse through his body, his face flushing and his palms wet. His head was spinning. The memories were just the start of it. She was so familiar, but she was also so dif-ferent. Why did he think closure was possible? That anything about this relationship and the way it had ended was the kind of thing that could be resolved? That there was a version of the universe where she could forgive him?

"You're not fine. I'm going to stay here with you until someone else comes. Call your mother. Call someone. Call a friend."

"My mother died."

Teddy swallowed. "I'm sorry. I didn't know."

Rosemary had hated her mother. She had emigrated to the United States when she was seventeen, pregnant with Rosemary, and unsure of the identity of the father, after being kicked out of her home, a rural village in Russia. The two most likely contenders for fatherhood, her mother claimed, were a soldier who had passed through their village on leave and had promised Rosemary's mother to take her out of the rural town and into Moscow, where she could have a better and more interesting life, but after they had been intimate, which was apparently part of the deal, the soldier left in the middle of the night. The other possibility was a cousin who had been abusing her since childhood. After the soldier abandoned her, Rosemary's mother took matters into her own hands and hitched a ride into Moscow, and through a series of complex events, eventually made it to America. Her life had always been very difficult, and she never let Rosemary forget this, mostly by hitting her and insulting her throughout her childhood. Despite the fact that this was a clear reaction to trauma, from a child's perspective it was hard to navigate the relationship, and the mother and daughter hadn't gotten along very well, particularly when Rosemary became old enough to acknowledge the patterns and defend herself with awareness and psychology.

"It's okay. We weren't close. You knew that."

"I know. I'm still sorry. I'm here now. I'm not going anywhere."

"Is that supposed to mean something?" She had turned her face away from his. She closed her eyes. "I'm tired. I'm going to sleep for a little while."

"I'm here if you need me," Teddy said.

"I won't."

"I'm still here," he said. And he smiled. Why did he smile? It felt trivial and stupid. She didn't smile back.

He took the train back to Brooklyn rather than an Uber. It reassured him that she hadn't changed. Her refusal to back down when she had an idea or point of view attracted him to her in the beginning, and she wasn't intimidated by him simply because he was older. He didn't like to date younger girls, although many of the guys he was friends with from college and his abandoned graduate degree were always trolling the bars around NYU and the New School, looking for college girls impressed by AmEx cards and UberBlack, the way older men with disposable income could cover a $100 tab and afford a car back to Brooklyn to show off a fancy apartment in a new and poorly ventilated high-rise in Williamsburg where the dishwasher was always broken no matter how many times the super came to fix it. A lot of his friends in their late twenties and early thirties loved these girls, but Teddy had always felt like talking to them was like talking to a parrot—flashy colors and eye-catching plumage, but ultimately they could only repeat back whatever you said, and if you threw a cover over their cage, they would disappear. You could stop texting one of these girls for months, and then they would show up at your place at 3 a.m. at the drop of a "u up?" text. He was looking for someone who had a personality and a point of view and honestly, some self-respect. Someone whose life didn't revolve around what bar they were going to hit this weekend and how to match their eyeshadow to their shoes after watching endless TikTok videos.

Rosemary was engaged with the world, engaged in literature and art and music and history, and after a few conversations with her, it became clear that she was much smarter than he was. She made references that went clear over his head. She was twenty-four, and he was about to be thirty, but she knew art history in detail and could quote dates with remarkable accuracy, and he was the one who had attended art school. She was always reading. Sometimes it was avant garde poetry created using Google Search algorithms and artificial intelligence, and sometimes it was ancient Sumerian mythology. She wasn't too interested in movies or television and had problems sitting still to watch anything for an extended period of time, but if they kept a conversation loosely following a movie and she could ask questions or look things up on her phone, he could show her his favorite films. He could teach her about typography and the intricacies of the evolution of the printed word. She picked ideas up quickly, and she always wanted to learn. She was independent, and she didn't need him to be happy, which was why the fact that she had allowed him into her life was so monumental. He had been chosen. For a long time, this was an honor, but then it was a burden, and now he wasn't sure what it was. Once she had asked him if he was happy, and since he couldn't lie to her, he didn't answer, and that was the beginning of the end. He didn't say anything, and for her that was answer enough.

When he had first gotten the call, he had texted Elizabeth with a brief explanation of what was going on. When he got into bed, she rolled over and made a groan of acknowledgment.

"I'm back," he said.

"What's going on?"

"My ex-wife," he said. Elizabeth knew about all of this. "She was in a car accident, and I'm still her emergency contact. I think I'll visit again tomorrow."

"Why?"

"She doesn't have anyone else, I think. Maybe coworkers, acquaintances, but her mother died, and she's never been the kind of person who makes a lot of friends." He pulled the blankets closer around him. Suddenly he was very tired. It was almost two in the morning. "You've never been married."

"Okay," Elizabeth said. She wrapped an arm around Teddy. "Just let me know if I can help."

Her breathing slowed, and Teddy knew she was asleep again. He was happy with Elizabeth, happy in this bed, happy with his life. He didn't want to go backwards. He liked where he was. But he needed to close this chapter if he was going to keep moving forward in a healthy way. He needed to close it for good.

"I love you," he said to Elizabeth. But she was asleep, so really he was just saying it to the empty dark.

*

She was more alert when he visited the next afternoon. The doctors said two more days and she could go home. Maybe one day if the abdominal healing continued as rapidly as it had been. Rosemary had always been into healthy food and fitness, and she was in great shape, so that was probably good for healing. Teddy was much more sedentary, and this had always been a point of contention in their relationship. He didn't like sports, and he didn't like kale or spirulina or all that shit. He didn't eat red meat, but he drank a lot of beer, and he was an on-again, off-again smoker, and he had gone through periods where he had had an issue with stimulants, either prescribed or off the street.

These days he was doing a little better, not so much beer, better sleep schedule, and keeping away from drugs other than the occasional hit from his weed vape pen before bed. He was drinking tea instead of coffee and trying to walk more, and even swimming laps at the local pool, where Elizabeth got a plus-one on her gym membership, in order to get a little bit of cardio. He and Elizabeth were planning a camping trip for her thirty-sixth birthday and doing mushrooms in the woods with some of their friends. Elizabeth was good like that; she knew how to hit the balance between work and play. She helped him be a better version of himself, and in return he made her laugh, he found her little random presents, he tried to make her life silly and fun and happy. It was a good thing they had, and slowly he found that he could breathe again. God, did this mean he was finally growing up? The thought scared him.

"What are you doing here?" she said.

"I came to visit you," he said. He set his jacket on the chair next to her bed and sat down. She flinched at his proximity to her. The bruises on her face were purpling.

"I don't want you here," she said. "I thought I made that perfectly clear."

"I was worried. I thought I'd just do another check."

"I don't want you to check on me," she said. "You're not a part of my life anymore."

"I still care about you," he said. "I never stopped. Aren't I allowed to care about you?"

"Please, stop," she said. She had been tough, mean, but he knew her, and he knew she couldn't do it forever, especially when he was standing in front of her. Her voice had cracked. She was looking at the window even though the blinds were drawn. There was another bed in the room, but it was empty. Teddy went and sat on it, trying to get physical distance while still close enough that they could hear each other.

"I don't want to talk about this."

"We should," he said. This energy was flowing through him, a powerful kind of courage. He had waited so long to apologize, to make it right. "I was so fucking scared, Rose."

"Why are you here?"

"To tell you I'm sorry," he said. His face was wet, but his words were clear. "To tell you how fucking sorry I am." There it was. There was everything he had never said, distilled into one sentence.

"Sorry isn't good enough," she said. And she wouldn't say anything else. She wouldn't look at him.

*

They had called. It was two years ago, but he would never forget it. The divorce papers had just been finalized. The hospital had called and said his wife was hemorrhaging and he was her emergency contact and he needed to come, but he had gone out and gotten drunk with his friends. She had called him again and again. At first it was because she wanted him to come, but as the days passed, the calls became angrier, and the voicemails were at first desperate, then confused, then hateful. Then they stopped. He put the pieces together and understood; she had miscarried. He had never responded to any of it. He had ghosted, disappeared, never apologized or said anything. He was a piece of shit and a coward and a deadbeat, he had tanked his marriage because he didn't want to be responsible, he wanted life to be easy and it wasn't, he was a horrible, shitty person and he knew that, and now everyone knew it too. He just wanted life to be simple. That was it. He didn't deserve Elizabeth, and he hadn't deserved Rosemary. And he hated himself.

"Why are you here?" It was his third and final visit. He had left that afternoon and walked around, considered getting drunk, and decided against it. That wouldn't help anything. All roads, it seemed, led back to the hospital. To Rosemary.

"I don't know."

"You do."

He couldn't lie to her. Actually, no one could lie to her, but that wasn't the point.

"You were supposed to be here," she said. "When I had the thing. I called. The hospital called. Everyone called. You didn't come. You were my emergency contact."

"I'm here now," he said.

"It's not enough." There was a finality to her tone.

"I'm so sorry." The walls were breaking down. The building was falling down. They were surrounded by the rubble of their lives. Light fixtures crashed down and shattered. Cinderblocks narrowly missed Teddy's head, and pipes broke, spraying water everywhere. Alarms began to go off. Around them, people were yelling, but Teddy couldn't hear anything. Windows were blasted out, and the glass was everywhere in shards. Bricks broke in half as they exploded out of their mortar placements. The toilet fell five stories. The elevators crashed down their shafts after the cables snapped, and the filing cabinets were all knocked over as papers floated past them like birds or butterflies, but they were now the only two people in the world. Sirens sounded in the distance. The dust made it hard to breathe, but there wasn't much to say anymore because it was all almost over.

"I'm sorry," he said.

"It's not enough," she said. Somehow he knew that, but he had tried anyway. It wasn't enough, it wasn't and it never would be.

The Dark Room

THE DESERT IS graceless, unspecific. The sun beats down on Lucy's head. The house is an old Victorian, out of place among the New Mexican pueblos, low-lying houses the color of sand and brush, that populate this area. It's on a chunk of land the size of a high school football field. It's a twenty-minute drive out of town. Andrew drives, one-handed, his mechanic's blues rolled up around his elbows, in his 1994 gray station wagon. He loves that car more than anything. Lucy sits in the passenger seat, smoking a menthol cigarette, getting smoke in the car. She waits for Andrew to say something about it; he never does.

The house is an urban legend. Trinidad, Colorado, is one of the most haunted places in the Southwest. Kids avoid the house. They give it a wide berth. Teenagers come here to have sex. And, lately, people have been coming here in pairs, older people. Couples. "It's a transcendent experience," Andrew said when he was explaining it. He had some friend at work who had done it. "You've done acid, right? It's kind of like that."

Lucy has never done acid. She took a lot of Vyvanse in college. Andrew knows this about her. He knows everything about her, or at least he's supposed to. They've had the requisite conversations. They've been together a year, an awkward collection of Chinese dinners and okay sex on the couch during commercial breaks. Together is a relative term. To Lucy, it means, "I went to tell you first when something good happens." To Andrew, it means: ?

"It'll be great," Andrew says, taking Lucy's hand.

She has no choice but to believe him. When he first brought up the idea, she said, "Hell, no." It sounded like a nightmare. It sounded like a nightmare of nightmares.

But three days ago they were shouting outside of a barber shop.

Andrew: You don't love me. You don't even know me.
Lucy: Oh, I know you, all right. I know you too well.

This trip is supposed to bring them back together. Not that they're apart. No one wants to say that. No one wants to think that.

"It's supposed to bring you closer to the other person," Andrew said when he was convincing Lucy to go. "You get totally sense-deprived, and all you can think about is the person you're with. Some grad students at the University of Colorado set it up."

No one has lived in this house for a long time. Lucy can see that. She can hardly imagine a troop of graduate students, armed with blackout curtains and duct tape, descending on the place. But crazier things have happened. Like, for example, a year ago, when Andrew leaned back on the hood of his gray station wagon and said, "Lucy. Do you want to go out with me?"

He was a friend of a friend. All of her girlfriends had said he was trouble, not the bad-boy-dangerous-motorcycle-driving kind of trouble she was used to, but a different, unspecified kind of trouble, the kind of trouble that lurked behind doors and appeared when you least expected it. He was cold. People noticed that about him. He was logical, almost to a fault. He read economics textbooks for fun. He could argue with a brick wall if the brick wall hinted that it might argue back. He's twenty-five but acts seventeen or thirty-four, depending on the day. He has no plans for the future. He doesn't want kids, doesn't want to get married, doesn't want to live together. He didn't seem to want anything, except in those fraught particular moments when he wanted Lucy desperately.

Lucy knows all these things about him and more. She keeps them filed away in a special part of her brain, the part that deals with difficult emotions. She looks over at Andrew, who is chewing on the inside of his lip. It's hot, midday. This was when he could get off work.

Something clicks. She pushes him up the porch steps, hands on his chest. "Lucy," he says reproachfully. "Lucy, don't."

There is no one around. A car passes lazily down the block, slows down, and then keeps moving. She kisses the spot where his neck meets his shoulder. Andrew makes a noise, his back to the house. "Stop."

Andrew has this idea that Lucy uses sex to distance herself because she doesn't know how to relate to people on a fundamental level. Lucy does not agree with this idea. Lucy slips her hands inside Andrew's shirt, feeling his skin. He tastes like blood and metal.

"I don't think this is going to help anything," Andrew says.

"It's not going to hurt either."

"I said, no."

Lucy pulls back. Her hair is heavy on her neck, wet with sweat. "What's wrong?"

"Nothing's wrong. I just want to get this over with."

"You're the one who wanted to—never mind."

Andrew takes Lucy's hand again. "Come on. Let's go. We said we were going to do this, and now we're going to. Don't you want to?"

Lucy wants to go home. She wants to sleep for a hundred years. She never wants to speak to Andrew again.

She can never say no to him. "Fine," she says.

Andrew opens the door to the house.

A cavern opens before them. The first thing that hits is the smell. Grandmother's basement, mold. A black cat screeches and runs down the stairs. A rafter is coming down from the kitchen ceiling, and the linoleum is peeling. Dust covers every surface. No one has lived here in a long, long time.

"Where are we going?" Lucy asks.

"We should do the speed first," Andrew says. "Before, you know. We can't see. Or, I don't know, whatever you want to do."

"No, you're right."

They pick through the detritus and cut through the kitchen to the living room. Piles of newspapers fill every corner. There are old books, phone books, strange collections of ceramic artworks, rotting paintings, and other junk shoved underneath broken tables and chairs. In the living room, three squashy orange velvet couches surround a low-lying coffee table.

"How are we going to measure time?" Lucy says.

"I brought an alarm clock," Andrew says. "I have water too. And there's a bucket in the room. That's what my friend said. In case—you know."

Lucy nods, trying not to think about it. She takes solace in the fact that Andrew won't be able to see her, doing whatever it is she needs to do.

In front of the couches, there is a busted flat-screen TV. Another cat yowls and runs into the other room. Andrew puts his backpack down on the coffee table and spills out the contents. First there are the orange pill bottles, the legal stuff—Adderall, Ritalin. There are four tabs of Xanax, for the comedown, in a little plastic baggie. Then there's a gram of cocaine. Then the yellow-white crystal with a little glass pipe.

"You don't have to do it if you don't want to," Andrew says. "I just thought, you know, if we're going to do this, we might as well go all out."

"And this is what your friend did?"

"Something like this," he says. "I don't really know all the specifics. I just know that him and his girl were fighting all the time, and now they're totally good."

Andrew and Lucy have been fighting all the time. Three days ago, outside of the barber shop:

Lucy: I don't know why you insist on arguing all the time.

Andrew: I'm not arguing. You're arguing. You're the one who always does this.

Lucy takes one of the orange pill bottles, shakes out four pills, and swallows them with a gulp of water. Together they make short work of the drugs. She doesn't touch the crystal in its little plastic baggie. Andrew turns the pipe over, his eyes focused, and she can see the change in him immediately. She uses her expired student ID to tap out lines of cocaine on the coffee table and does them. Her brain starts making a sound like ticker tape.

"Your nose is bleeding," Andrew says.

Lucy rubs her nose hard and fast. He passes her a tissue. "Thank you."

Everything looks sharper. She has more ideas, not all of them good. Andrew kisses her, his mouth cool. His pupils are pinwheels. She used to like that about him, the way his blue eyes showed her everything. Now she doesn't know how she feels.

Together they ascend the stairs. Slowly, as not to fall through them.

"You ready?" Andrew says.

"I'm ready," Lucy says, although she has never felt less prepared for anything in her life.

"Okay," he says, and together they open the door.

This was Andrew's idea. Everything is always Andrew's idea—where they go to dinner, what movies they see. It was Andrew's idea that they go out in the first place. He has friends at the University of Colorado, psychology department. A bunch of burnouts, just like him. Lucy doesn't like his friends, although she would never say that out loud, even to herself. Andrew is a good man, he has a steady job at the collision shop, but most of his friends are perpetual grad students messing around in people's brains and getting whacked out on drugs.

"I don't do that stuff anymore," Andrew always says, but Lucy knows he does, and more often than he'd like to admit. She's seen him on ecstasy, crystal, coke, not every day, not even every week, but enough to know that he's still a part of that world. She doesn't mind. He's an adult, and he can do what he wants. But she hates that he lies to her about it.

These psych majors had this idea, Andrew explained to her over dinner a few weeks ago, that if you could put someone in a sensory deprivation chamber, but also fill them with stimulants, they would totally lose their mind. "Because there would be no stimulus," he told her. "Do you get it? You'd totally turn inward, and your brain would, like, explode."

"Wouldn't that make more sense if you did it with, like, acid?" she said.

"Everyone's done LSD experiments," he said, making a dismissive gesture. "This is a whole new thing."

It turned out that two of the students who went to this abandoned house to set up their very own sensory deprivation chamber were in some kind of nasty fight about a girl. They ran the experiment on themselves. Apparently, the combination of the drugs plus the lack of stimulus allowed them to speak candidly about their problems in a way that they never would have been able to on the outside, and they came out best friends.

"It's kind of a double-edged sword," Andrew said. "One time, two people started fighting, and one guy totally bit the other guy's ear off. But usually, it works."

"Because doing speed makes you think you've got some kind of clarity?" Lucy said, confused. She was stuck on the idea of someone's ear getting bitten off.

"I guess so. I mean, what's clarity," Andrew said. "If not a state of mind?"

"Can't we just go to couples therapy?" Lucy said.

"Couples therapy is for married people," Andrew said.

"I don't think that's true," Lucy said. "Otherwise, they would call it marriage therapy."

"You're being pedantic," Andrew said in a way that made Lucy sure that the conversation was over.

The room is smaller than Lucy thought it would be. The windows are the first thing she notices. They are covered in cardboard, duct taped, and hung with blackout curtains. There are three mattresses on the floor, no sheets. There's a dresser on one side of the room, and this is where Andrew places his water bottle, his backpack, and the alarm clock.

"If anything, we can feel our way over here," he says.

"Right," she says.

The point is the darkness. The point is finding one another again. The point is finding each other in the dark.

"Should we do it?" Andrew says. "Turn off your phone."

Lucy does. Andrew takes her phone and puts it in the backpack, then does the same with his own. Andrew messes around with the alarm clock for a minute.

"It's set."

"Don't screw it up. I don't want to be trapped here forever."

"You're not going to be trapped here. The door isn't locked. You can always leave."

"No one knows we're here. We could die here. We could kill each other."

"Are you planning on killing me?" Andrew gives Lucy a look. She realizes that his face might be the last thing she ever sees.

"No," she says finally.

"Well, all right then." Andrew turns off the light.

The darkness is different from what Lucy thought it would be. She's been in the dark before. She's from the suburbs, outside of Philly—came to Colorado for graduate school, master's in education. It got dark there, real dark. She did summers in Cape Cod, and she remembers turning off the lights and being enveloped in darkness. This is different. Her eyes don't adjust. Not for a long time. The darkness is a living thing. It takes a while before she says anything. Maybe five minutes.

"Are you still there?" she says.

"Of course I am," Andrew says. "Where would I be?"

Those Cape Cod summers, lying in the dark, Lucy used to wonder if the darkness could hear her. Now she knows it can. The drugs are making her want to move, but there is nowhere to go. She can't see the walls, doesn't know the confines of this room. The mattresses on the floor make it impossible to walk around. She sits down, drumming her fingers against the softness of one of the mattresses.

"Come here."

"Where is 'here'?"

"Here."

She reaches out, finds a shin, a thigh, a belt buckle. Stomach, chest. "Hey."

"Hey."

She can feel his breath, warm on her face. "We could finish what we started downstairs, if you want."

"If you think that will help anything," he says. "Besides, that will take up, what, twenty minutes? Is that really what you want to do with your time in here?"

"Not if we do it right. Twenty minutes." Lucy laughs. "Come on."

"You're doing it again," Andrew says. "You're using sex as a defense mechanism."

"You're the one who wanted to do this."

"And you're the one who said we needed to talk." Andrew shifts underneath Lucy's weight, pushing her halfway off him.

Lucy thinks again of those Cape Cod summers and the way the darkness felt complete around her, like it was holding her close. Now someone is holding her, and she feels alone.

"We do need to talk. But I would rather do other things instead."

Three days ago, outside of the barber shop, people had stared at them:

Lucy: We need to talk. We can't just not talk about this.

Andrew: We're not going to do this in public, Lucy.

Andrew puts his hand in Lucy's back pocket. She wriggles at the touch. "You know what I want to talk about," she says. "You don't have to say anything if you don't want to. You know how I feel."

"I know."

She exhales, frustrated. It's typical of him to shut down at a moment like this, when they are supposed to be figuring things out. It's typical of him to believe that there's some kind of quick fix, some kind of easy way out. But isn't that what she believes too? That they can just have sex, and suddenly it won't be over? She pushes her hand down his chest, undoing his belt buckle in one smooth motion.

"Luce." His voice holds everything in it. She moves her hand, and he inhales. "Don't stop."

"I know," she says. "I know, I know, I know."

In the dark, it's easier. It's easier to move and not think. There is fumbling, but it doesn't matter. Some things don't work properly—they've done an awful lot of speed. But they are together, and they know each other well. This is something they can do. This is the only thing they can do.

Lucy finds herself thinking of nothing but the blackness, bright and alive, sparking in front of her vision. Shapes shift and move in front of her eyes. Her mind supplies stimulus where there is none. Every nerve ending in her body feels like it's on fire. The denim of Andrew's clothes grate against her bare skin. The stubble of his chin rasps against her face.

When it's over, they lie half-undressed and fidgeting, trying not to move, because there is nowhere to go. Neither of them wants to untangle from the other.

"It's not enough," Lucy says.

"What do you mean, it's not enough?"

"I told you I loved you," she says. "And you said, 'why?'"

"Well, I want to know why," Andrew says.

"What, do you want a list?"

"Yeah, make me a list."

"I'm not going to make a list," she says. She wipes her hand on his thigh. "I just do."

"That's not enough either," he says.

"Then, what?"

"I don't know," he says.

Outside of the barber shop, three days ago. Andrew had just cut off his shoulder-length hair, and Lucy had come to pick him up.

"Do you like it?" he said, smiling.

"Sure."

"You hate it," he said, and there was malice in his voice. Lucy was never sure which one of them was picking the fights. Maybe it was both of them. Maybe it was neither. Maybe the fights were picking themselves. Maybe they were under the surface, waiting. "You hate it, and you never want to speak to me again."

"You'd like that, wouldn't you?"

He made a mock-angry face. "Of course not. Come on, let's go. I'm hungry."

"I almost don't recognize you," she said. It was the wrong thing to say. She knew that, and she said it anyway.

"In a literal way or in a spiritual way?" he said, a mean edge to his voice.

She had told him that she loved him the week prior. He had said, "Why?" Since then, they had been circling each other like cats, baiting and biting, waiting for the other to strike.

"In any way," she said.

"Lucy," he said. "Let's not do this here."

"Where should we do it then?"

"Literally anywhere else." He paused for a moment. "The dark room."

He had brought up the dark room idea before. He thought it was interesting. He would take any excuse to do drugs. She was desperate. They would never sit down and have a real conversation otherwise; she knew that. They would start drinking instead. It would devolve into a screaming match.

"Okay," she said. "Let's do it."

"You'll do it with me?" he said.

"I just said I would."

It wasn't her idea of a good time. She didn't like uppers, didn't like drugs in general. She was afraid of the dark. But she loved him. "I would do anything for you," she said, and it sounded like a lie in her mouth.

"I know that," he said. But he didn't say anything else.

The darkness is everything. Lucy feels like the room has expanded to the size of a small cave. Her eyes have finally adjusted, and there are crags and stalagmites everywhere. Bats flutter in and out from in between the walls. She jumps from mattress to mattress, having kicked her shoes off. They have been sacrificed to the dark room. She will never find them, not until they turn the lights on, but somehow that doesn't matter. Andrew is somewhere in the room, but that doesn't matter either. She jumps and jumps until she hits a wall and bounces off, falling to the ground.

"Shit."

"Are you okay?" Andrew says.

"I'm fine. I just fell."

His hands find her body in the dark. She wants nothing more than for him to hold her and tell her that everything will be fine. But it won't.

"You're never going to say it, are you?" she says.

"I don't know," he says. "I don't think I feel it the same way you do."

"What does that mean?"

"It means, of course I care about you," he says. "I would help you bury the body. I would make you breakfast. I would bail you out of jail. But—I don't know. That's a big word. I don't really even know what it means."

Something snaps. "I want to get out of here."

"We've only been in here—oh, I don't know. Not long."

"I want to go." Suddenly she wants nothing more than to be out of this place, back out in the world where there is light and brightness and space. "Let me out. Where's the damn light switch?"

His hands release her. "Fine," he says. She can't tell if he's disappointed that the experience is over or that they are. Are they? She isn't sure. She can almost make out his figure in the dark as he gropes for the light switch. "Close your eyes," he says. "This is going to be a shock."

On the car ride home, Lucy's head bumps against the window. She doesn't feel like smoking now. She's taken the Xanax, and it came on strong, like a sword slicing through clouds. She feels woozy and sick. Andrew drives, one-handed as always, his driving hand languid on the steering wheel. The desert bleeds by. Nothing registers. It's not a long drive, but it feels like a long time before Andrew pulls up at Lucy's apartment building.

Part of Lucy wants Andrew to stay, to come upstairs. Part of her never wants to see him again. She thinks about the logistics of it. They have a lot of the same friends. They go to the same bars. She's plotting his death when he asks, "Are you okay?"

"I'm fine."

"Do you want me to come up?"

"Whatever you want."

"Let me just find parking," he says.

Lucy gets out of the car, unsteady on her feet. She walks up the stairs. Inside the apartment, she peels off her clothes, which are soaked in sweat, and leaves them on the floor in the kitchen. She starts the shower, turning the water as hot as it can go.

She gets into the shower. Andrew knows where the spare key is. The water pounds into her skull, breaking it into little pieces. She doesn't feel better, but she doesn't feel worse. Somewhere in the distance, she hears Andrew knock on the front door. He knocks again, louder. She hears him banging on the door. She doesn't know why he doesn't use the key. She keeps waiting to hear his key in the lock. He sounds desperate. He hits the door louder and louder. She doesn't get out of the shower for a long, long time.

We're Not Cat People

LATE LAST NIGHT I had the dream again. The one where they dredge the lakes and find Tia's body, looking up at me with its blank eyes. I'm tired of waiting. She's been dead twelve years.

Jon wakes me up because I've been screaming. "It's okay, it's okay," he says. "It's not real. It's just a dream." But it's never just a dream. It's always something more. In the morning I read the papers, and some girl in another county has taken a cattle brand to her stomach. That small body pinched out by red-hot pokers. I don't know how to tell Jon I understand how that feels. I don't know how to tell Jon anything these days. The rot has devoured the tree. I have an addiction to stories like these.

"You're just going through a transitional phase," Jon says before he leaves for work. "You'll feel better in a few weeks."

He's right. Jon is almost always right. It's one of the things I love and hate about him. He's a Capricorn. Slow and steady, an earth sign. He's my rock. I don't know what I'd do without him, but sometimes I look at his face and think, I can't do this. We're getting married in the fall.

He didn't know about the dreams when I met him. They started when I was a child. It's not prediction, exactly. It's more that I dream about the past. I dream about what could have happened, and sometimes the past is worse than the future. But I can't tell that to Jon, who is so beautiful and eager, so full of hope and love and impossible promises.

I'm waiting to hear about jobs. In the daytime, I putter around the house and check my email obsessively. I'm a librarian. I've applied to all the libraries in the area, and now I'm just waiting to hear back. I've gone on some interviews, and they always say, "We'll get back to you," but I've been waiting four weeks, and no one has. Jon is a lawyer, and I don't really have to work, but I want to, and not working has made me vacuous and strange. It's not good for me to do nothing. Jon knows this, and he gives me projects: a bird house, fixing the gutters in the house, but it's never enough. It never fills all the empty time between when Jon leaves for work and when he comes home.

The only thing that haunts this house, these days, is me.

This morning I'm scrapbooking—taking all the old photos of Jon and me and putting them in an album for us to look at when we're old. It makes me sad and nostalgic, to look at all the old photos of Jon and me—so young, so carefree—glued down on the pages. I get into a funk and have to lie down for a few hours with the television on in the background. I would call a friend, but Jon and I have just moved to this neighborhood, and I don't really know anyone here yet. I don't feel lonely, in that I don't mind being alone, but there's a part of me that misses having people to talk to.

Tia would know what to do on days like these. She was the energetic, fun one. She was the one who would say,

"Let's go on an adventure." And we would—to the mall, to White Castle for burgers, to the movies in the middle of the day. When she died, a piece of me, the piece that did spontaneous things, died with her. Sometimes I think it was the best part.

Around three, I take a walk around the neighborhood. It's a typical cul-de-sac, houses in neat rows, manicured lawns. I don't know why Jon wanted to move here. I would have stayed in the city, but Jon said if we were going to be raising babies, if we were going to be putting down roots, he wanted to do it in the suburbs. I didn't care much either way. I would follow Jon to the ends of the Earth. If he said he wanted to raise his children in Hell, I would buy some suntan lotion. Sometimes I think my dependence on him is too much. It's encroached on my own personality. Sometimes I think I'll look in the mirror and find nothing left of myself. But then he'll embrace me, and I'll remember my own body, and everything will be all right.

I find the cat by the side of the road. It's been hit by a car. I hear it mewling and go to see what's happened. It's only been run over a little bit—its leg shattered—and it's in a lot of pain. I run back to the house and find a cardboard box and scoop it up, and then I call a vet's office.

"I have this cat," I say. "It's been run over by a car."

"Your cat has been run over by a car?"

"No, not my cat," I say.

"Not your cat?"

"Just a cat."

But already it's my cat. It's looked me in the eyes, it's claimed me.

I drive with it in the front seat in its cardboard box. At the vet they tell me they'll have to amputate the foreleg, and just like that, I have a three-legged cat. It's an orange cat, orange and white. They ask me its name, and I say, "I don't know."

"Think of something," they say. "You have to give it a name."

I think of the girl, the cattle poker. "Tia," I say. "Its name is Tia."

Tia was my cousin. She died the summer when I was eighteen and she was seventeen. She walked into the river that ran behind our house with stones in her pockets. They found her body in the lake that the river fed into three weeks later. Before that she was just missing, and we could have hope, but I knew from the moment she didn't show up for our family movie night that she was gone; I could feel it. I don't know how, but I knew, I just knew. I didn't have to dream anything. It was just a feeling. She didn't leave a note. But all the neighborhood kids knew why she did it. We just didn't tell anyone. I wanted to tell her mom, but her sister, Alma, also my cousin and a year ahead of us in school, made me promise not to. "You don't need to smear her name anymore," she told me. "You don't want her to be remembered as emo *and* a slut."

Jon is angry when he comes home and sees that we have a cat. The cat lies, sedated, on the bed I've bought for it, at my feet.

"We aren't *cat people*," he says. "We're dog people. We're outgoing. We want kids. People with cats aren't like that."

"I think we could be cat people," I say. "Besides, it's so lonely at the house without you, when you're at work. This way I have a friend."

He gets angrier when he finds out what I've named the cat. "You named the cat after your dead cousin." His voice is almost a shout. "Don't you think that's a little bit morbid?"

"The Jews name children after the dead," I say.

"We're not Jewish."

"It's a pretty name," I say. I look down at the cat, sleeping peacefully. "Just let it go, Jon."

He huffs and puffs all the way up to bed.

Gradually, though, Jon warms to the idea of the cat. At first, he won't let her sleep in our bed, but after a few weeks, she's sleeping on his pillow more than I do. She squeezes in between us and takes over the whole bed and even relegates me to the smallest amount of space in the corner by the edge of bed. I hear Jon talking to her in the mornings when he's feeding her. "Who's a good girl? Do you want some num nums?" It's adorable, frankly. I start to make friends with some of the women who live on the street, and for a little while, it seems like things are getting better. I don't have the dream for two weeks in a row.

Then Alma calls and tells me she's coming for a visit.

That's what Alma is like. She doesn't ask if she can visit, she tells. I love Alma, but I don't particularly like her. At my and Jon's engagement party, she got drunk and cornered Jon in a bathroom and tried to kiss him. Later she said she was doing me a favor by testing him to make sure he was really dedicated to me, making sure he was a good guy. He did the right thing, which was to immediately push her away and then take her downstairs and get her coffee and water and tell me what had happened. After that I said she couldn't stay at our house anymore, and our moms got involved and had to broker peace between us. But for months I had dreams that Jon would leave me for her, that he would cheat or who knows what else, and I woke up in a cold sweat and had to make myself Sleepytime tea and watch reruns of *Law & Order: SVU* until I could fall back asleep on the couch.

We have a guest room in this house, and she knows that, so I can't exactly turn her down, but part of me wants to tell her to stay at a hotel. "It'll be good to see you, Alma," I say through my teeth when she tells me the date she'll be arriving. Two weeks. She says she needs to pass through on business. I'm pretty sure this isn't true, but I don't question her because I know it will cause even more issues. But I'm anxious when I tell Jon about it, and he grimaces and asks if I can make some kind of excuse. We brainstorm but can't come up with anything that sounds legitimate. I feel nervous as her visit comes closer. I'm still jobless, and I'm still not settled in our new house or our new neighborhood. I'm still not unpacked, and I still don't know where Jon has put all the kitchenware. I have to keep calling him at work to find out where he's put things like the blender or the can opener. I don't know if I can put up with two weeks of Alma.

She arrives on a Wednesday in a haze of perfume and silk scarves. Alma works for a department store, and she always has samples of fragrances and clothes to share. Over the years she's been promoted from retail at the makeup counter, and now she's a buyer and travels to meet with wholesalers. She always makes these trips into some kind of vacation even if they're just boring work trips to flyover states, stays in drab motels. She has a way of making the best of everything. I'm not much of a shopper, but there is something fun about the way she bestows gifts upon everyone. For Jon, she has a new tie. For me, a new blouse, in a splashy color I would never have picked for myself but that actually looks nice with my hair color. On Wednesday night, the three of us stay up too late drinking champagne and then whiskey, and Alma tells us about her string of lovers as Tia the cat curls up at her feet.

"I can't believe you got a cat," Alma says. "I never figured the two of you for *cat people.*"

"I didn't think we were cat people either," Jon says. "But the cat finds you."

He sounds wise when he says this, and we all sit and think about this for a moment. Then everyone bursts into a kind of hysterical laughter.

We haven't told her the cat's name. Part of me thinks she'll be honored, and part of me thinks she'll be offended. She, Tia, and I grew up together in the same suburbs outside of Chicago. We were neighbors, and we all played together, soccer in the street and princess dress-up at each other's respective houses. We drove each other around in our parents' cars when we were old enough and covered for each other when we wanted to go out with boyfriends. Then Tia killed herself, and Alma and I sort of grew apart, as if Tia was the glue that was holding us together. Alma went off to college, and I did the same a year later. We got different kinds of jobs and friends and lives and slowly lost touch. Alma lives fast and parties hard, and I've never felt as if I have that much in common with her. Tia was dreamy and introspective; she was more my speed. She understood about the dreams, and Alma never could.

"So when are you making with the babies?" Alma asks. "You've already got the house and the pet. I figure it's just a matter of time."

"We're practicing," Jon says. I hate it when he does that, speaks for me. "We'll have them when it's time."

"You're not getting any younger," Alma says. "Jeez. I can't believe we're already thirty."

"Don't remind me," Jon says, sinking lower into his whiskey glass. He's got the flushed cheeks that let me know he is very drunk and very soon he will start admitting secrets about either me or him that I would rather him not. "Damn, I'm scared shitless. We're getting married, Alma."

Jon and I have been together for six years since a mutual friend introduced us. I was living in Portland completing a research grant, and he was waiting to take the bar. It was a blind date. I liked his quiet, understated sarcasm and his ability to make the simplest tasks into wild adventures, cracking jokes all the way, terrible puns and random facts that made chores feel like games rather than an obligation. He treated everything like a learning experience, and everything he did, no matter how random or tedious, was meaningful, something he could do to the best of his ability and gain a valuable skill or experience from. His approach to life was about making the best of every situation. I was in a hole where I buried everything I felt and distracted myself with intensely detailed archival work. Meeting Jon was like defrosting. Slowly I found myself thawing and becoming a human being again, and he was patient with me.

He believed in what I had to offer the world, and he wanted to be there with me when I figured out what that was.

He had also spent enough time with my family, including Alma, to be honest enough about these kinds of personal topics. Babies, marriage, that kind of thing. We'd spent more than one night getting drunk with my various cousins. He came from a very small East Coast family, only child, no siblings, no cousins, just a single mom and a half-brother, much older, no dad to speak of. He liked my family because there were a lot of us scattered around the country and we were all doing different things.

I can see from the way Alma is shifting in her seat, the flimsy barstool in our kitchen, that she is just as drunk as Jon is. I'm drunk too, I realize, the whiskey making my head swim.

Alma coughs. "I hate your stupid fucking happiness."

"Oh, don't be like that," I say. "From what you've told us, your life sounds fabulous. I just sit around the house all day, waiting for a job that never comes."

"You think I don't want what you have?" she says. "Stability? I'd give my left nut." She goes to the window to light a cigarette—we've told her we don't want her smoking in the house, but she's ignored us—and pulls the window open. "You're living the dream, you two. Even this stupid fucking cat."

Tia, the cat, blinks an eye as if she can tell she's being talked about.

Jon opens his mouth and then closes it again. Then he opens it more definitively. "I'm scared. I don't know if I'm doing any of the right things or if I'm doing them because they're what everyone else does. I love Lynn, I do. But of course—what if love isn't enough?"

"It's all we've got," Alma says wisely, cigarette smoke curling around her like some kind of perfume. "It's all we've got."

And the three of us sit in silence until Jon announces he's going to bed.

That night, liquored up and full of disquieting conversation, I can't sleep. I wake up, and for the first time in weeks, I pace the quiet streets in my bathrobe and slippers, walking up and down the cul-de-sac under the orange of the streetlamps. Jon doesn't know I do this. I like the absolute silence, save for the fuzz of someone's television, the hum of the generators, the occasional hiss of a car as it passes by. I wonder if this calm, this quiet, is what Tia felt in the moments before she decided to end her own life, walking at night through the woods, stones weighing down her pockets, a modern day Virginia Woolf. After she died, I poured through her journals, trying to find some sign, but I knew the reason. Everyone did. It was all any of the kids in our neighborhood talked about for months.

About a month before she killed herself, Tia had gone on a date with one of the running backs from the football team. He had gotten her in the backseat of his pickup truck and raped her. She told her sister, who told me, who told my friend Sadie, who told the rest of the school. She never told an adult, never told a counselor, never told a teacher. As far as any of the adults in her life knew, she was a happy teenager, if a little withholding, a little withdrawn, in the month before she died. Of course there were rumors. That she was easy, that she would give it up to anyone. But they were just rumors. Whatever the rumors, the shame, the violation, was too much for her. She never confronted her rapist. She never pressed charges. She went to the river instead.

After she died, girls stopped going out with that running back. He was shunned. His friends stopped talking to him. He was kicked off the football team because people refused to practice with him. There were never any formal charges called, but his life was effectively ruined. It wasn't justice, not by any means, but it was something. I've long since forgotten his name. I'll never forget Tia's name, not as long as I live.

The dreams are more than I can handle, and at a certain point, I admit that it's not that I can't sleep, it's that I'm afraid to.

There will never be any justice, Alma said to me once. It was one of the only times she's ever spoken to me about her sister. She was right. Some wounds will never heal, no matter how carefully we clean them, and wait, hopefully, for them to disappear. A scar can indicate that something has happened, but an open wound signals something else entirely.

I let myself back into the house around 5 a.m., when the sun is just starting to come up. I'm surprised to find Alma sitting in the kitchen with a cup of coffee clutched between her knees.

"You're up early," I say.

"I always rise early," she says. "Got to get the day started."

Without her elaborate makeup, with her hair pulled back, she looks younger. More vulnerable. "Is there coffee for me?"

"I made a whole pot."

It occurs to me that Alma and I will have to spend the whole day together. I pour myself a cup of coffee and dump milk into the mug.

"Where were you?" she asks me.

"Just walking. To clear my head. I couldn't sleep."

"Ah."

"I still have the dreams," I say. "About her."

"I don't."

In my whole life, I have only told four people about the dreams. The first person was my mother. I was very young. She told me that my imagination was very good and that it meant I was going to be creative. When I got a little older and tried to explain the way they tended to involve real people and alternate timelines, she took me to a therapist, who diagnosed me with ADHD and wanted me to take a low dose of Prozac. The pills stopped the dreams, but they also made me feel like a zombie, and I stopped taking them without telling my mother. I was twelve or thirteen. My mother kept filling the prescription, and I kept telling her I was taking them, and I stopped telling her about the dreams. When I went to college, I said I didn't think I needed the medication anymore, and because I was an adult, she didn't argue, and we never talked about it again.

Tia knew, and I think she had the same kind of ability, but we never talked about it directly. It was just something we shared, a language that we could both speak without confirming that we both spoke it. I know Alma sometimes felt left out in the way we were with each other, but I sometimes felt left out when they played together, and the bonds they shared as sisters were different than the ones between Tia and me, and I couldn't access either of them in the same way. The three of us were involved in a triangle of push and pull. When Tia died, I tried to talk to Alma about the dreams, and she knew what I was talking about, but she would never reference it directly. So I stopped mentioning it.

Explaining it to Jon was difficult, but all I told him was that sometimes I had vivid nightmares about people I knew, and it felt as if I was engaging with possibilities that hadn't happened but could happen, different forks in the road, different versions of myself. A kind of backwards fortune-telling. "The brain is powerful," he had said originally. "More powerful than we know." He was interested in hearing about the dreams, and he could usually calm me down when I was scared. He could keep me connected to this version of reality. He was my anchor. I depended on him more than I wanted to admit, but I knew he depended on me too.

Alma could sometimes be caught in the right mood and say cryptic but revealing things about her sister or her childhood, but she isn't in the mood, it's clear. But I press the subject anyhow.

"It's been twelve years," I say. "You'd think I'd be over it by now."

"I know how long it's been," she says slowly.

"I guess it's not something you really ever get over."

Alma turns sharply to face me. "She was my sister," she says. "Of course I'm never going to get over it."

"Look, I'm sorry—"

"Lynn, don't." Alma exhales. She stands up. "I know you want to play happy housekeeper and make everything suddenly better for everyone, but there are some things you just can't fix. Okay?"

"Okay." The word tumbles out of my mouth before I can stop it. "I'm sorry."

"Don't be. I'm going to take a shower."

And she leaves me sitting in the kitchen, feeling sorry for myself. Unable to move forward and unable to look back.

I find Jon later. Alma is somewhere else in the house, and we're talking in hushed voices so she doesn't overhear us. We're hiding in the bathroom off the master bedroom, and Jon is running the shower to cover the sound of our conversation. It seems like overkill, but I've learned from experience that Alma has surprisingly keen hearing.

"She doesn't hate you," he says. "She's just moody."

"She accused me of trying to fix her," I say. "I just want to talk to her about Tia. She's the only one who remembers her like I do. So what if I want closure? That's a natural human response."

"You're going to have to work this out on your own," Jon says. The shower is filling the room with steam and making me sleepy. I haven't really slept well in several days. Anxiety gets to me whenever I lie down and close my eyes.

"I'm here to support you, of course, but you need to pinpoint what you need, what will make you feel like these feelings are resolved, and then you need to do whatever that is."

"I hate it when you're right."

"I hate it when you know I'm right and you're going to ignore my advice anyway." He kisses the top of my head. "Now, I was actually going to take a shower. You can join me if you want, but I was going to do that, and if we talk any more, I'm going to be late for work."

It doesn't take much though. It's a kind of unraveling, and once the thread has been pulled, it all begins to fall apart.

"You know," Alma says one night at dinner. "I guess you really are cat people."

"I guess we are," Jon says.

"I'm just realizing," Alma says. "I've been calling her 'cat' this whole time. Does she have a name?"

Jon looks at me. I look at Jon. "We've been calling her Tia," I say slowly.

Alma's fork clatters to her plate. "What did you say?"

"I said we've been calling her Tia."

"You named your cat after my dead sister." She doesn't say it like a question. She says it like a statement. She's stopped eating, and now she has her elbows on the table and her hands together in a kind of grasp. I think about the best way to explain, and nothing comes to mind. The explanation sounds stupid. Everything I could say sounds stupid. It's all a web of bad decisions, bad dreams, and it's on the verge of becoming so tangled that I can't make sense of any of it, let alone explain it to anyone else.

"We were at the cat hospital, and they asked me, and it was the first name that came to mind, and I thought it would honor her," I stammer. "I didn't mean any offense by it."

"You named your cat after my dead sister," she says again. "You named your cat after my dead sister."

"I just thought—" I say, but there's nothing, nothing I can say.

"I need to tell you something," Alma says. Her voice is like ice. Colder than ice. Ice can melt, but this is entirely different, and it signals a kind of pain that runs deep. "Something I've never told anyone else before. But I need whiskey first."

I don't say anything, but Jon knows to pour from the good whiskey that we only drink on Christmas. For himself, he only pours a little, but for Alma and me, he pours a double shot each. He doesn't sit by me in the living room; instead he joins Alma on the couch.

"What I'm about to tell you might hurt," Alma says. She takes a swallow of liquor and then exhales.

"Okay," I say. "You know you can tell me anything."

The words feel hollow in my mouth. There may have been a time, when we were children, when Alma could have told me anything, but that time is passed. We haven't shared secrets in years.

"You know Tia killed herself," she says. "But you don't know why."

"I do know why," I say. "It was because she was—assaulted. By that football player."

"That's what people thought," Alma says. "That's what everyone thought. But that's not what happened."

"What are you talking about?" I say. "That's exactly what happened. That's what you told me."

I can imagine the scenario perfectly: Alma, whispering to me, cupping her long-fingernailed hand around her mouth to amplify her voice. *That boy forced himself on Tia.* My look of shock and horror.

"I know that's what I told you. That's what I told everyone. Because I didn't want people to know what really happened."

"What really happened?"

I look at Jon. He's clearly uncomfortable. I told him what happened to Tia a long time ago, when we first started dating, and he's never really liked talking about it. Jon is one of those people to whom nothing really bad has ever happened, and he doesn't know how to deal with the big stuff.

But he smiles at me all the same. It's a weak smile, but I know he supports me, and I know he's trying. And that's what keeps me going. With that I know I will be safe no matter what bomb Alma is about to drop.

Even so, I'm not prepared for what she says.

"Tia was never raped." Alma's voice is a whisper. "I was."

"What?"

"I'm the one who went on the date with that football player," Alma says. "And Tia walked in on him. Raping me.

Hurting me. She stopped him. And she took the blame for it. She was a good sister."

"Why would she do that?"

"She just did. She wanted to. She didn't want me to suffer."

I thought of Tia, her daydreamy, soft personality. She wasn't tough like Alma, hard-hearted. I couldn't imagine her making a choice like that, to take responsibility for another person so wholeheartedly. To shoulder the blame, to wear the stigma, the scarlet letter, the rumor mill churning. And at the same time it made sense—she was always the one bandaging our skinned knees and elbows, putting lotion on our sunburns; she was the one who took care of us. Without her, we had to take care of ourselves, to varying degrees of success.

"She really did that for you?"

"She did. And in the end, it was too much for her. Too much of a burden to bear. I've never understood—why she did it. I've never been sure."

"It's easy to romanticize, I suppose."

"She was a better person than I was. I always wished it was me who died, not her."

Jon flinches. "Don't say that, Alma."

"It's my fault she's dead." Alma takes a sip of her whiskey, winces. "It always will be."

"Alma."

"What? It's the truth."

"She made her own choice. Sometimes people do. It's just the way life happens. You can't stop it." I can feel myself trying to convince her otherwise, but at the same time,

I blame myself too. I blame myself for not being able to stop her. "We'll always blame ourselves."

"I don't know." Alma looks misty. "And that fucking football idiot just gets to live his life."

"It's not fair."

"Life's not fair." She laughs, a harsh sound. "Anyway, now you know. What a day."

Part of me wishes I didn't know. It doesn't change anything, and yet it changes everything.

"It's going to be okay," I hear myself saying. "We'll all be okay."

My voice doesn't sound like my own. I've dreamed this over and over. I don't know what the truth is, and I don't know if the truth matters. I don't know anything. Who am I supposed to forgive? Who am I supposed to mourn, and who am I supposed to love? The past and the present are colliding, and I can't make sense of any of it.

Alma leaves on a Saturday. The last few days she was here, I avoided her. I didn't try to hide it; I turned up the radio when she came into the kitchen, I pretended to be asleep on the couch when she walked into the living room. I straight up left the room if I could make up an excuse. Tia the cat followed me around, mewling, hopping around on her three legs. I don't know how to process the information Alma has given me, and I don't know how to process the guilt. If I had done something differently, if I had asked the right questions, if I had seen the signs. There were no signs. I think of the girl with the cattle poker yet again. The things we do in desperation.

"I'll see you soon," Alma says when she leaves. "Call me."

But we both know I will do no such thing. Jon might; he's better at keeping up with family than I am. I'll leave that up to him. When she's gone, the house is eerie and silent without the music of her voice. The cat liked her, but after a few hours of wandering around and meowing, she finds a new spot on the heater and curls up and seems nonplussed.

We're not children anymore. We're adults. As children we competed for each other's attention and love and admiration. But we loved each other, or I thought we did. We didn't love each other enough to protect each other from the world. To confess and share and overcome stigma or shame.

When Alma leaves, Jon and I don't know what to say to each other, but I know he will protect me, and I know that whatever dreams I have, he will make sure I'm safe. I'm lucky in that way, to have found someone like him, someone who will make sure that when the past threatens to overcome the future, he will help me navigate the murky waters. That night, I fall asleep on the couch with my head on Jon's chest. His even, steady breathing soothes me. For the first time in a long time, I don't have any nightmares. I don't dream of the past, and I don't dream of the future. I don't dream at all. Silence is not enough, and neither is fear. My daughter, who is already growing inside of me, will not be afraid to speak up, even if I can't protect her from everything that can hurt her in the wide and scary world. But I can do my best to help her navigate. Alma will help and Jon will help and Tia the cat will help, and we will tell her about cousin Tia as well. My job at the library will allow me to give her all kinds of books and all kinds of perspectives. I hope she doesn't dream of the past. I will do everything I can to make sure she looks forward to her limitless and powerful future.

I Love You Like a Brother

MY FATHER'S FUNERAL was on a Monday. I paid the director by check and walked into the funeral home. The caterers were sending everything to the house. The house I would have to sell, now that my father was dead. I hadn't spoken to my father in four years. Not since he told me that if I wanted to move to New York, be an artist, I was dead to him. Okay, I said. I guess I'm dead to you then. He still spoke to my brother, Grant, who would be here before the funeral started. Grant was two years younger than me and a doctor in Los Angeles. Obviously my father liked him more than he liked me. My father was ex-military and a hardass. I hadn't missed him once we stopped talking.

Coming home was like trying on clothes from high school—I was relieved to find out they still fit but also somewhat horrified to think I could still be that person. If I wanted to. If I just changed a few things about my life.

But I wasn't. I was thirty. And maybe my plaid skirts and Siouxsie and the Banshees T-shirts still fit, but I was not the same person.

I supposed I was sad that my father was dead though. He had driven my mother away. I didn't know where she was. I didn't know how to get in contact with her, tell her he was dead. Maybe she was checking obituaries, and she would see. And come. I hoped, vaguely, that this would happen. I knew it wouldn't. Likely she was in Florida or something, someplace warm, not thinking about us.

The funeral home was depressing. Poorly lit. It smelled of formaldehyde. People would start arriving in half an hour. I had elected for a short service, the shortest possible. My dad hadn't been particularly well liked. He was a tough man. But he had friends, drinking buddies at the bar, and they would show up. Then they would descend on the house for the wake, get plastered on Jim Beam, and fall asleep on the couches, leaving me to clean up.

I wasn't looking forward to this day. I guess no one really looks forward to their father's funeral. But I was particularly apprehensive.

"Sara," someone said. I turned. It was Grant. He looked older. I hadn't seen him in person in two years, although we talked on the phone every few weeks, texted more frequently than that. "You look good."

I was wearing a too tight black dress, heels. "So do you."

He looked tired. He was in his last year of residency at the hospital. Neither of us had been able to get away when we had heard Dad had a heart attack—Grant, because he was working; me, because I didn't want to.

"Let's get this party started then," Grant said. "Put the fun back in funeral."

I smiled, despite myself. Grant could always make me laugh. He was my baby brother.

"Who do you think is going to show up?" he said. "Eric?"

My blood ran cold. "I doubt it."

"He could. We ran the obit in the paper, like Dad wanted. He could have seen it."

"I highly doubt Eric reads the local paper."

Still, I had thought about it. From Facebook, I knew Eric had a wife and a two-year-old, that he seemed happy. We had broken up when I had gone away to college, RISD in Rhode Island. We had still seen each other for birthdays and Christmases, up until I moved away for good four years ago, after the big split with my dad. In those four years, Eric had gotten married, had a kid, started building a life for himself. A life without me.

I didn't know what I would say if he showed up. "Sorry for leaving?" "How dare you move on?" "Are you happy?" Nothing seemed right. Probably I would just stand there, dumbfounded, until he walked away.

"You never know," Grant said. "It's a small town."

"Don't I know it."

Someone walked through the doors, and Grant went to greet them. I stood by the photograph of my dad, feeling inadequate. It was a feeling I was used to. More people started coming through the doors, and I exhaled slowly. I just had to get through this day, and then I could pack up the house and leave this town and never, ever come back.

The wake was an absolute disaster. All of my dad's drinking buddies brought whiskey, and no one touched the plate of bagels the caterers brought. They just kept drinking until they couldn't see straight and sprawled out on the couches telling stories about my dad that I really didn't want to know, disgusting stories, while Grant and I tried to keep straight faces and took turns going outside to smoke cigarettes. Leaving these men alone inside our house invited the fear that they might break something.

About an hour in, it got even worse. Owen showed up.

"Sara. It's good to see you."

I was already incredibly drunk. "So," I said, feeling the meanness creep into my voice. "Your brother was too much of a little bitch to show up, huh?"

"I think he didn't feel it was appropriate for him to come today," Owen said. I remembered how much I had always liked Owen and tried to keep my composure. "Given all that's happened."

"Not appropriate," I said. "Is that his way of saying he doesn't want to see me?"

"I think that's his way of saying he doesn't think it's a good idea for you two to see each other," Owen said. "But I can't read his mind. I don't know everything he's thinking."

Owen was three years behind me and Eric in school. He followed us around everywhere. We taught him how to smoke weed, how to smoke cigarettes, how to hide it when you're too drunk to stand. He was like my little brother too. It was hard to see him like this.

"Not a good idea?" I said. "What does he think I'm going to do?"

"You know, he's married now."

"I'm not going to attack him," I said. "I have self-control."

"I can see that," Owen said.

"Don't be a fucking asshole."

I could tell I was swaying in my shoes. Owen looked at me, and I could tell he was judging me, wondering where the person he had admired had gone. I wondered what had happened too.

"I don't want to see him either," I said. "I don't have anything to say to him. But you know, there's a lot of things that happened that you don't know about."

Eric couldn't have told Owen everything that happened. There was no way. We had sworn to keep it a secret, punishable by death.

"I'm sure there's a lot about your relationship with my brother I don't know about," Owen said. "But that's between you and him."

"So tell him that," I said.

"I just came to pay my respects," Owen said. "This isn't about my brother."

"Whatever you say."

"I'm going to go now," Owen said. "I'll tell my brother you said hello."

"You do that. Actually, as a matter of fact, don't."

I knew I was being vindictive, but I couldn't help it. I hated Eric for not coming when I needed him more than ever. So what if he had a wife and a kid now? My father had just died. He should have known that I would need him. He should have put that aside.

I went into the back room and pulled out my phone. I still had his number saved. We had agreed to delete each other's numbers, but I never had. I thought about dialing it for a long time. Sitting in the dark, I don't know what happened, but I must have fallen asleep.

*

I dreamed of looking for something I couldn't find. When I awoke, it was dark in the house. Everyone had left. Grant was still awake, cleaning up beer bottles that people had left on side tables and end tables around the house.

"Are you all right?" he said. "You disappeared."

"I'm fine."

"I saw you talking to Owen. Did he come to talk to you about Eric?"

"Yes. No. I don't know."

"Sara," Grant said quietly. "What happened between you and Eric? That made you leave that last time? It wasn't just things between you and Dad. I know that."

"I can't—I can't talk about it. I promised Eric I would keep it between us."

It felt like a non-answer, and yet it was the truth. I didn't want to betray Eric's confidence, even though I wanted to tell Grant what had happened more than anything. I wanted him to understand. I wanted someone to understand. Even I didn't fully understand the choice I had made, but it's what I did. I had to live with it.

"All right," Grant said. "If that's what you want."

I went upstairs to my childhood bedroom, long ago converted to a guest room. I got ready for bed, even though I'd been sleeping for hours. I felt strangely exhausted. It had been a long day. As I was getting into bed, my phone rang, a number I didn't have saved.

I answered the phone. "Hello?"

"It's me. Come outside."

*

Eric was as tall as I remembered, his long blond hair tied back with a leather thong. His face was orange in the porch light, the hard planes of his cheeks brutal and unforgiving. He looked at me, and I could tell he was doing the same thing I was—examining the differences. I had stopped coloring my hair dark a few years ago and let it go to its natural brown color. I had stopped wearing my glasses and started wearing contacts. I was dressed for bed in a T-shirt and pajama pants, my feet bare. He was wearing a work shirt and jeans. He looked severe, as always. I had always admired that about him; his industry, his ability to look like a workman in any scenario. He was blue-collar, and I respected that. I was something else, and that separated us. In the end, it was what had pushed us apart.

"Sara."

"Your brother said you weren't coming."

"I had to."

"Why's that?"

"Your father died."

"I know."

He took a packet of Marlboros from his shirt pocket and offered me one. We smoked in silence for a few moments. "I'm sorry I didn't come earlier," he said. "I didn't know what to say. I didn't know what people would say."

"You didn't know what your wife would say."

"She doesn't know I'm here."

"No?"

"No." He blew smoke out of his nose.

"Why didn't you tell her?" I asked.

"I didn't know how to explain who you are to me."

"You can't just say ex-girlfriend?"

"You know you're more than that." He paused. "You are."

"I know." I didn't know what to say next, so I didn't say anything. I waited for him to say something.

"I'm sorry about your father," he said.

"We never got along anyhow."

"Still."

"I know."

He put his hand over my hand, a gesture that was meant to be comforting but came off as patronizing. He had never had a parent die. Now both of mine were gone. He had sat with me when my mother left, when I couldn't sleep or eat or do anything, and I had never thanked him, not once.

"I was just thinking about your mother," he said as if he could read my mind. "This isn't like that."

"No, it's not. I never said thank you for that."

"Yes, you did."

"Well, I'm saying it again." I searched his face for answers, for reasons why he was so cold and yet so familiar at the same time, and found nothing. He was a stranger to me now. We hadn't spoken in four years, and he had a wife and a child and a whole life without me in it. "Tell me about your baby."

"My son," he said slowly. "Yes. His name is Keith."

"You always wanted to be a father."

"Yes."

This admission brought an arc of pain so pure into my body that I nearly doubled over. "I'm sorry," I said. "I'm sorry I couldn't do that for you."

"It's okay," he said. "You had other things you needed to do."

"And I'm doing them," I said. "I just had my first show in New York."

"That's great then."

For another moment, we were silent. He flicked his cigarette butt away, and I did the same.

"If it had been a boy," he said, "I would have named him Jonathan."

"We never talked about names."

"I thought about it though," he said. "Did you?"

"I tried not to," I said. And I remembered the drive to the clinic, the way he had broken down and cried and begged me not to do it, the way he had asked me to stay, stay in town and be his wife, the way I had coldly shut the car door behind me and gone inside, and let them cut his baby out of me because I didn't want to, I was afraid to, I couldn't imagine the rest of my life as a wife and a mother to a man I wasn't sure I loved, to a man I desperately loved, when I wanted to be an artist, I wanted to make something of myself, I wanted to leave this stupid town and do *something*. Something else. I wanted to stick it to my father. I wanted to show them all. I couldn't let him trap me. I couldn't. "I'm so sorry."

And then we were both crying and holding each other, and I knew he could never tell his wife about this, there are certain things that married couples must keep from each other, just like there were things he and I had kept from each other, and I remembered the last thing I had said to him, which was "I love you like a brother," which was a lie, a deranged lie, for I loved him so much more than that, I always would, and I felt sick to my stomach. Had I made the wrong choice? We held each other and cried for a long time, grieving the life that never was. The life that he had built for himself in the interim loomed over us.

At a certain point, we separated. We didn't say anything to each other. He got into his car and drove off. And I went back into the house.

What Would Happen

DECIDING TO TELL the truth can be like trying to make a promise and then making a bunch of caveats. "I'll tell the truth, but only if you send me a self-addressed envelope, and it has to be postmarked October 15th, and the envelope has to have a cat sticker but not a cartoon one—a realistic cat—and also you have to send it on a full moon, and it must be raining." It's true that I had a plastic bottle of bourbon in my bag and I was nineteen, and it's true that the beers were drunk too quickly and that I was grading papers in the bar and that after we stopped seeing each other regularly I quit smoking.

It was a nonsmoking room, but Jay lit a cigarette anyway, dropping ash into a paper cup. I lit one too, but the taste of it made me sick; I had smoked too many already, they clogged my lungs. I put it out in the empty drink cup. Jay came over and sat next to me on the bed.

"I trust you," I said.

"I know," he said.

Later, I couldn't remember what I said after that.

The destruction came later. It was painful, but I was used to that. Pain was the easiest part of all of it. It took a long time to separate everything into what was okay and what wasn't. The truth was this concept that didn't really always make sense when you looked at all the events laid out in front of you. But I was sure of myself. And then Jay was in front of the counter at the ice cream shop where I still worked, with his wife and his two children, and he hadn't returned my emails in over a year, and I didn't know the words for how fucked up that was. The words would come later. The truth isn't something that can be explained, but the truth does exist, somewhere, even if we can't always find it or see it. It's there, and it can't always tell us much, but it's there, and I find this comforting as I tell this story.

I think I was a lonely child, but I didn't realize this until much later. In college everyone was always talking about roommates, but I found myself wanting to keep to myself. It was always fun to hang out in the all-night study room, and I enjoyed the parties on the weekends, trying to use our bad fake IDs to get into bars or purchase cheap liquor, but I always needed to be alone at the end of the day. I needed to recharge. I had lots of projects I wanted to focus on, research to do on subjects that interested me or books that I wanted to read. I valued sleep too, and my classmates were often griping about all-nighters, while I usually tapped out eventually and went to bed. I was always taking notes, and I had started writing poetry in high school with no real direction, just putting together images I liked, but writing wasn't a focus; I was a politics major as well as studying art history, and the academic workload was demanding. I wasn't trying to escape, but I wasn't trying to find myself either. I knew who I was, and I knew what I wanted. And then there was Jay, and then there was Julio, and together they broke it all down, and I realized I knew nothing and I never would.

It was the first week of sophomore year, and I had added a creative writing class to my schedule, thinking I would enjoy it, after feeling excited and inspired by the poetry seminar I'd taken in high school and the "Fiction of the 1960s" elective I'd signed up for and loved during my freshman year in college. Writers like James Baldwin, Ken Kesey, and Doris Lessing had encouraged me to think about fiction in a whole new way, and the poetry I'd read, from Ginsberg to Anne Carson, had unlocked new ideas about what poetry could be. Jay was commanding from the moment he walked into the room. There was a certainty to the way he carried himself. It wasn't the same as confidence. It was clear that he knew what he was doing, he was an expert, and we should feel lucky to be in his presence because he had so much to teach us, and I trusted that, even as I learned what a lie it was.

My mother blamed me, saying I encouraged him, made myself too available. But I think all I was, all I ever showed him, was how much I cared, how much I wanted to be good. How much I wanted to fit in, and since I would never fit in, I could compromise with excellence. If I wasn't going to be like everyone else, I could be so brilliant that they would all respect me, but in an entirely different way. And I think he got that. I think he got that because I think he felt the same way.

But what do I know, really? Speculation is a poor excuse for the truth.

*

Boundaries, it all comes down to boundaries. Rayna said to me once, "How do you always fuck such hot guys?" We were in the study room, and honestly, her boyfriend was lackluster considering how beautiful she is. I knew she was saying that, even if she wasn't saying it directly. We were all so glad she broke up with him when she did.

"It's about standards," I joked. "You gotta aim high." She and Alejandro had a thing, sort of, but I don't think anything actually happened. And I don't know what she's doing now. I don't even know where she is. After we all left the dorms, we spread out. We lived our own lives. And even if we stopped to talk in the halls, the intimacy was gone, the proximity. I kept going to Ale's parties, but it was hard to talk in any kind of real way with the music and the drinking and all of the sexual politics. It's amazing how you can know someone, love someone, and then life just ferries them away.

The night Michael died, I wanted to tell Jay. I don't know if I did, maybe I did. I wanted him to know that I knew what pain felt like. Over the years, we've been in touch sometimes. His own pain he's shared with me in a way that probably isn't fair or appropriate. But that's the way it is sometimes. Sometimes people just come into your life, and they don't break the connection or cut the cord, and the link is always there. His son liked the cotton candy ice cream, I learned, when the two of them came into the ice cream shop. He liked that flavor, too, despite the fact that it was bright blue. That was something that always made me laugh. The oddity and randomness of it.

*

Lucia is younger than me, but she's beautiful in the kind of way that makes me feel sick and good at the same time. I can't stop touching her. "It took me a while," she says, "to get you comfortable with me." She says this as if she's won some kind of prize. And maybe I've won a prize, but not for long, because she's already escaping my grasp and talking to another man, then disappearing downstairs and returning, rubbing her nose. I'm obsessed before I know I'm obsessed. I'm speaking Spanish and touching my hair.

Even years later I'm so easy to manipulate, and I know it. My own panic, my own need for attention, my own desire to be told how special I am, she sees it all. My inability to be vulnerable and my desperate need to be. Not many people read me so clearly and easily. I'm good at people, but she's better. The affection dries up as quickly as it begins.

"I'm okay," she says when I walk in and ask how she's doing. "It's been a shit day."

I'm sipping my first beer of the day and taking in her outfit, the mismatch of her bright orange tracksuit pants and baggy suit jacket, on top of XXXL-sized T-shirt advertising "Jennifer's Bat Mitzvah, 2013." Her lipstick is cherry red, and her curly hair is tied into Pippi Longstocking braids. "Shit day?"

"Just kinda having problems with a friend."

"Yeah, I'm going through some stuff with a friend as well." I'm thinking of Jay, but I don't know how to explain this. Now in my late twenties, Jay and I don't speak much, but we do exchange emails once in a while. We've known each other for almost a decade. I sent him a message recently giving him an update of my writing life, and he responded that his family has moved out of the city, which doesn't totally surprise me because he has two young sons now, but he finished his email by casually saying, "You should visit sometime!" This statement, somehow, has unraveled me, and I'm now a pile of yarn and emotion, disorganized and formless, unable to explain how I really feel.

Lucia is nodding like she understands. She grabs my hand. I can't figure her out.

I became aware of some things and not of others. Mackenzie was curled up in a bar chair, and I immediately remembered that she was twelve weeks pregnant. Like me she was inconsolable. At some point I held her. Schmidty couldn't stop pacing. Jonathan would sit for a while and then stand, and at one point he went down and yelled in the walk-in, which blunted the noise, but we could still hear it. [redacted] kept his hand on my back. I couldn't stand to see Jonathan cry; it made me even more hysterical. Apollo wandered around, trying to inflict his grief on others. I hated him then, more than I had before. For being a wreck and for not being strong in this moment when we all needed him to be strong. *You have a baby on the way,* I wanted to tell him, thinking about Mack. *Get your shit together.* But he was unintelligible and sobbing and grabbing people. I went outside and called my mother and told her what had happened. She didn't have anything useful to say, but I didn't expect her to. I just needed her to know.

*

People came in and out. Junior was wiping his eyes, and I wondered who had told him. I knew it was going to be hard for him since he came to X Bar almost every day to shoot pool. He and [redacted] shared a cigarette. We kept trying to remember who needed to be here, who we needed to call and tell the news. Eventually Devon and Zack were done talking to the cops, and they showed up. I'd had too many tequila shots by that point. Devon's face—it was too much for me. Her pain was like a lit match. I swallowed and felt myself caving in from inside, not sure I would ever be able to look at her again.

Will and Sophie walked in as [redacted] and I were leaving. There were hugs, tears, questions. This is where it gets blurry. No one seemed to have any information. We told everyone how much we loved them; this seemed very important. People were looking for pictures, but no one was telling stories yet. In the car I felt numb. Here were the facts: Michael was dead, and he would always be dead. Michael had committed suicide. The more I said it, the more I hated it. I wanted him to be alive, and he was dead. This felt unfair. I didn't know what to do. I didn't know if there was anything I could do. I didn't know how to keep going. There was nowhere to go.

"It has been decreed," Lauren had trilled, slamming her beer can down on the bar. She was laughing. She was still dressed for teaching, in a blazer and low-heeled boots. Jay had been stunned when he had seen her.

"What happened to the punk rock nineteen-year-old in my 'Intro Fiction' class?" he had asked her. "Last time I checked, you wouldn't be caught dead in a blazer."

"I have to dress the part," she told him. "My students can't know I'm twenty-three and out drinking on a Tuesday night."

"I guess you're right," he said, but he seemed disappointed, as if she had somehow failed him by growing up.

Stomping down Houston Street, Lauren felt her heart leap into her stomach. They were meeting at the Double Down Saloon, her pick. If she was going to burn down New York City, this was where she thought it should begin. They would zigzag across the city, she figured, ending up somewhere in Brooklyn. Or not. Who knew? She couldn't stop thinking about the conversation they'd had when they were first writing up the contract.

"If we were to go on a rampage," Jay had said, taking serious sips from his wine glass, "you know what would happen."

A chill had run up Lauren's spine. She had never thought of Jay *that* way. He was in his late forties, and her professor besides. "I don't know what you mean," she had said.

"Well, you *know*," he had said, making meaningful eye contact with her. "You know what would happen. But I don't want that to happen," he had said. "Because I respect you too much. We're friends, and I want us to stay friends. If something were to happen, we wouldn't be able to stay friends."

"We're friends?" Lauren had said.

"Yes," Jay had said. "Of course we are. Look, now I've upset you. You won't even look at me."

"I'm not upset," she had said. "I'm sorry." She didn't know why she was apologizing. She hadn't done anything wrong.

"I'm sorry too," he had said. They were both silent for a while.

She was slightly worried, she had to admit. They had had fun that night, drinking beer and wine at some bar in Crown Heights, his pick. It was near his home; he had made time for her in between his packed schedule of teaching and writing and taking care of his two children, ages two and six. They had been trying to see each other for months, but it had never worked out. She had had so much to tell him. About teaching, about graduate school—which he had pushed her to apply for and even written her a recommendation for—about writing, about life.

"I got broken up with this week," she had told him when he sat down on the barstool at the end of the bar.

"Are you grading papers?" he had said. "Is that what you're doing right now?"

"Yes," she had said, sweeping her students' work into a folder and sticking it in her backpack. "I do most of my grading in bars. I expect you can relate."

"Hey, something about the lighting, it really helps," he had said.

She knew he would never judge her. So she told him about her breakup, about her grad school classes, about the way her new professors were pushing her to do the best writing of her life.

"I don't want to be pushed," she had said, laughing. "I want to be told I'm perfect."

"I never even told you that," he had said. "I pushed you, didn't I?"

"Of course you did," she had said. "But you also always told me I was great. I'm great, aren't I?"

"You are," he had said. And he had smiled.

But then things had taken that turn. She hadn't been expecting it; never in a million years had she ever thought that he could potentially be attracted to her. There was the gap in their ages; twenty years, at least, and the fact that he had been her professor, besides. She had never been attracted to him. Their relationship had never had a whiff of that, even though they had always been close. She told him about the petty disturbances in her life: the breakups, the professors who slighted her, the academic advisor who bullied her, the parents who were having a hard time grappling with her ambition. He had shared some things with her as well: a difficult moment in his career, a problem with his editor, issues with his tenure. But there had always been a professional distance, or so she had thought. Now that she thought back, they had always been closer than a typical student-teacher relationship, but that was what the mentor-student relationship was all about, wasn't it? Especially in writing, where the subject matter was so personal, so intimate?

He had been there for her during some of the most difficult times in her life. Some crippling depressions, some stunning manias. He was the first one to say, "You seem a little off today. Are you okay? Are you taking your meds?" He was the one who had made her pinky-swear that she would stay alive to see her first book come out. However long it takes, he had said.

And he had always pushed her to do her best work. She felt safe with him. Or she had. Now, walking down Houston Street, she didn't know what to expect. It had started off as a joke: "Let's burn down the city." He had always had a streak of anarchism in him, maybe more than a streak. They had always had fun drinking together. Maybe that's all it would be, she thought hopefully as she turned on Avenue A.

She trusted him with her life. She would have done anything for him. She looked both ways before crossing Houston Street and stomped out her cigarette butt on the corner. She took a deep breath. The double doors of Double Down Saloon loomed in front of her.

Jay was sitting at the bar in the front, drinking a whiskey. "I said tequila," Lauren said, already glad that they had something to talk about. "Why aren't you listening to me? It's literally written into the rules. If we break one rule, we'll end up breaking them all."

"This rule we're going to bend," he said. As usual, her old professor had his sunglasses on inside. He wore the kind of lenses that transitioned from dark to light when you came inside, but his evidently had not transitioned back to regular glasses yet. "I submit to the committee that we can change this one rule."

Lauren pretended to think about it. She had a copy of the rules in her backpack, and she took them out, along with a pen, and made an addendum. "Fine," she said. "But everything else stays.

"Okay," he said. They stuck out their hands and shook on it. Then they signed the contract. Jay's signature had a flourish to it that Lauren wasn't expecting.

Double Down was a large bar with a backyard that was closed even though it was almost summer. The front was cavernous with a pool table and a collection of booths, and in the back, it was tighter, closer, with tables and chairs for large groups to cluster. The walls were covered in graffiti, and pornographic movies played on the various screens mounted on the walls. Signs advertising $4 "Ass Juice" hung over the bar itself, a mystery liquor Lauren had never tried. She ordered a tequila shot and a Miller High Life and drank the shot and bit into the lime, letting the juice fill her mouth.

"So what were you thinking?" Jay said. "Did you have a plan, or were you just going to see how things went?"

"Well, I had a few ideas," Lauren said. "But really, I was just going to see how the night went."

"Night?" Jay said. "I've cleared my whole weekend."

Lauren laughed nervously. The night they had made this plan, she had joked, "We'll have to plan it for May, when I'm crazy again." But she didn't feel crazy at all. She felt frighteningly sane. The craziness came in waves, weeks where she didn't sleep and drank like a fish and smoked like a chimney. Her doctor had a word for it. And he had meds for it too, which she didn't always take. But lately she had been taking them, and she didn't feel quite unhinged enough for this particular excursion.

Jay seemed on edge, nervy, paranoid, too excited. "My wife thinks I'm visiting my brother in Boston," he said. "I haven't spoken to my brother in six months."

"She doesn't know that?"

"She doesn't know anything."

Lauren tapped her fingers on the bar. This was not how she imagined her life would be going when she had walked into Jay Gaines' "Intro to Fiction" class four years ago. God, had it been four years? It seemed like so long ago. She had walked in, thinking herself a big shot, and he had knocked her down a few pegs.

But first, they had bonded. Over what? She couldn't remember. What she remembered was him asking her to stay after class. "I need to speak to you about your first assignment," he had said.

"Was there something wrong?" she had said. She knew she wasn't a bad writer. She hadn't been serious about writing back then. She was a political science major. Wanted to go to law school.

"Nothing's wrong. Hang on a second." He was waiting for the classroom to clear out, until it was just the two of them, and the TA, who was hanging back, presumably to meet with him too. She had liked the TA; they had become friends later. "Nothing's wrong. It's just—you're exceptional."

"Excuse me?"

"Your work. It's exceptional."

"What?"

She had been so flustered she had left the room without saying thank you or goodbye. She had called her mother and told her what he had said. She had been elated—someone, and not just anyone, but a professor, thought her writing was good. She carried the feeling around with her all week, buoyant.

She had apologized, the next week. Stayed after class again, hung back. "I'm sorry," she had said. For being rude, she had said. "Thank you."

"Of course," he had said. "You said you're a politics major? Well, you should be a writer. Fuck politics."

"What?"

"Be a writer," he had said.

And four years later, she was in an MFA program teaching her own creative writing class. She didn't know how it had happened. She had put her nose to the grindstone. With his support, with the support of her parents and her peers, but mostly with that voice in her head—"you're exceptional"—to motivate her.

Their relationship had expanded. To talks after class and during breaks. He had asked her to be his TA. She had, the next year, been his TA. She had ended up taking a lot of responsibility in the class, teaching mini-lessons, making rules for the students. He told her she was the best TA he'd ever had. They had ended up getting close. He had told her about some things from his past, about his mother. She had told him, well, everything. About her ups and downs. About the bad thoughts, the ones that came at night. About the panics and manias. About what the doctor said. About the diagnosis.

He had been there for her. Through everything. He had been steady, unwavering. He had known what to say, what to do. She could never repay him for his kindness.

"You don't get less crazy as you get older," he had warned her. "I'm just as crazy as you are."

Now she felt like she was taking him up on his challenge.

The world was alive. Abuzz. She drank some of the bourbon from her water bottle and winced as it went down. They smashed their beer cans together. They had been drinking steadily at Double Down for the last hour, three beers down the hatch, vodka shots for Jay, tequila for Lauren, lime clinchers. She hadn't been drinking water.

Lauren felt strong, invincible. She wouldn't let her mind drift. Jay was rambling about something, and she focused on his words: the sound of his words, not what he was actually saying. He was lecturing, falling into teacher-speak the way he always did if you left him alone for too long, and Lauren could feel him slipping away from her.

"Do you see what I mean?" he was saying.

"No," she said and burst out laughing. "I don't."

They had been making a list of writers with mental health issues. Sylvia Plath, David Foster Wallace, Ernest Hemingway. She had an idea that she wanted to only teach bipolar writers in her next class, and he was helping her come up with more material. They were laughing. She felt refreshingly normal, even though she was on her way to drunk. It felt good to be sitting here, with someone she most certainly adored, talking about her favorite subject.

She felt some of the old mania welling up again, the old excitement. She bit her lip and sat on her hands to keep them in check.

"David Foster Wallace was the most successful when he was taking his meds," Jay said. "Just you remember that."

"I know, I know."

"I just worry about you."

"Don't worry about me. I'm fine."

Jay took out his pouch of rolling tobacco and started rolling himself a cigarette. He looked at Lauren. "Do you want to get out of here?"

"And go where?"

"Anywhere. The movies. The circus. I don't know. Let's walk up to Tompkins Square Park."

They walked out into the darkness. It had gotten dark while they had been inside; Lauren blinked in the light of the street lamps. They walked up Avenue A, dodging masses of summer people swarming in and out of bars on the avenue: the Library, Berlin, Niagara, Sidewalk. Jay lit his cigarette; Lauren followed suit. They talked about nothing, about Lauren's classes at NYU, about Jay's students at Columbia. They were just scratching the surface. Lauren could feel it. There was more that bubbled underneath, unsaid.

"I have something," Lauren said when they sat down on a bench in the park. "For us. If you want."

"What do you mean, you have something?"

They were passing her bottle of bourbon back and forth. Quickly, the bottle was getting lighter and lighter. The city was simmering, the May heat of the day dissipating. It was getting cool. Lauren pulled the sleeves of her hoodie closer around her.

"I'm so proud of you," Jay said suddenly.

"Right now?" she said. "Right now, you're proud of me?"

"Yes," he said and didn't explain himself further. "What do you have?"

She rummaged around in her backpack and pulled out the bag. Mushrooms, in a plastic sandwich baggie. "Shrooms. Have you done these?"

"Jesus," he said. "Not since—well. Not for a while."

"I thought it might be fun. Just take one—you won't really trip that hard. And the alcohol will counteract the effects."

His face flickered—a series of emotions she didn't recognize. "Give me one."

She reached into the bag, pulled out a mushroom, and handed it to him. His fingers closed around hers.

"You have to really chew it; otherwise they don't work. And they taste terrible."

They sat on the park bench, chewing furiously for a few moments. Then they both swallowed.

"How long?"

"About an hour."

"What do we do for the next hour?"

"I say we find another bar."

They found themselves at a hole-in-the-wall, drinking tequila (for her) and vodka (for him), limes for both, talking to the bartender. He was interested to hear that they were both writers.

"We're on a trip right now," Lauren informed the bartender. "We're doing a trip, and we're going to write about it."

"What are you going to write about?"

"Well, we're going to burn down the city of New York and write from the ashes."

The bartender laughed nervously. "Don't start at this bar," he said. "I really need this job."

In about an hour, colors started to look brighter. Then they started to shift and change. "Are you seeing this?" Lauren said. Her pupils were like disks. She couldn't see Jay's eyes behind his sunglasses. The neon signs behind the bar were moving and changing. The music was alive. "Look at this."

"I see it," Jay said. He looked slightly green, like he might throw up, but he also looked astounded. "I see everything."

Lauren sat back in her chair. Her whole body was vibrating. She could feel everything acutely; the wood grain of the bar was moving underneath her hands, and the stool underneath her legs was wobbling. Sounds were louder, but also softer. They had a quality that she couldn't quite describe, a kind of newness, a kind of being that seemed more real than anything she had ever heard before. Her whole body flooded with endorphins. In the center of the bar, there were a few scattered people dancing.

"Dance with me," she said.

"Oh, definitely not," Jay was saying, but she was already up and out of her chair, marveling at how everything glowed. Her hips swayed and moved to the music. Jay stayed awkwardly on the sidelines, quieter now, out of lecture mode. Lauren could feel him watching her. She wondered how lucid he was and how the mushrooms and music were affecting him. She gestured to the bartender for two more shots and slammed her shot, the taste of which was now marvelous and complex and almost over-whelming. The lime exploded on her tongue.

Magenta and cyan offshoots ping-ponged from the edges of objects. Neon looked magical. Wood grain swirled and flowed. Her pack of cigarettes looked friendly. The walls were breathing, but it was a gentle kind of breath, and she wasn't worried about it. She wasn't worried about anything at all. Tears came to her eyes, and she found herself crying, although she didn't know why.

"Why are you crying?" Jay asked.

"I'm just so happy," she said.

"I am too," he said. And took her hand.

And they danced together for what could have been three minutes, but could have been three hours, moving close together and then farther apart, because distance didn't seem to matter anymore. They became one being, with arms and legs that found each other and then moved apart again, and his hands were on her waist and then not, and his hands were in her hair and then not, and floods of what must have been euphoria (for there was not another word for it) went through her body, and she thought of everything that had ever happened to her, she thought of walking into his class for the first time when she was nineteen years old, she thought of teaching her own class on Monday morning, she thought of sitting in that bar with him as he said, "Well, you know what would happen," and thought to herself, is this it?

They would not kiss, not until much later. But she reveled in the knowledge that it would happen, that everything that would happen after was an inevitability, that it was bound to happen, that there was nothing she could do but lie back and let it go forth. She reveled in the power that she now held over him, and he reveled in the power that he now held over her, and they knew that they had broken the rules of the contract, but they didn't care, everything was clear, and then everything went black.

The last thing Lauren remembered was stumbling drunk and high on mushrooms into the hotel room, which Jay had put on his credit card, laughing that his wife never checked the statements anyhow. And it was a sobering thought, his wife and his two children, ages two and six, but she pushed them out of her mind and tried to keep from laughing as the hotel clerk (slicked back hair, maroon blazer) asked them questions about how long they would be staying and if they had any luggage, which of course they didn't except for the backpack and the empty bottle of bourbon.

Jay broke into the hotel minibar as soon as they were in the room and made them both a drink, which Lauren drank greedily, sucking down the tequila and ice as if it were her last meal, which perhaps it was. She was suddenly awkward, suddenly shy as she sat on the bed.

"Should I turn off the lights?" she said stupidly. Of course not.

"Leave them," Jay said. "We're just drinking."

She dreamed that she was back in Jay's "Intro Fiction" class. She had been slow to warm up to him, the way she was always slow to warm up to teachers. They had to earn her respect. Nothing was a given. She hadn't taken a writing class since high school and worked hard on the assignments, which was exactly why Jay had told her, "You're exceptional." But in those first few weeks, she had been mystified by this man who seemed so sure of himself, so confident, so secure of his place in the world.

Later she would find out it was all an act, and Jay was a mess of insecurities, paranoias, and needs just like she was. He could never sit in a room with his back to the door, for example. His mother was a paranoid schizophrenic, and he had certain tics, certain tendencies, that made her think he had inherited some of that disorder as well. But this gave him complete and total sympathy to mental health issues. Jay was an obsessive, just like she was. He was an empath too. He cared about each and every one of his students and tried to reach each one on their own terms.

Lauren had been resistant to this technique. She talked back in class, made jokes, but also flexed her academic brain, answered questions in her loudmouthed way, making sure he knew she was the smartest person in the room. But he had broken her down, slowly but surely. She remembered the moment when she had realized he was someone worth knowing.

He had been teaching a lesson about character. They talked about what makes a well-rounded character, what makes a strong character, details, everything. They built their own character on the board. As usual, she was hungover, barely taking notes. But then he asked a question to the class. "What do people talk about?" he asked.

Everyone had been stumped. What do people talk about? She thought about it. She didn't know.

"People talk about themselves," he crowed. He seemed very pleased with himself.

She laughed out loud. Yes, they do. He was right. This professor might know something, she remembered thinking. He was breaking down the barriers she had worked so hard to build between herself and other people.

In the dream, though, the classroom was melted and twisted. He was speaking about narrative structure. Jay was larger than life, in full lecture mode, saying, "Do you see what I'm saying?" the way he always did. She didn't catch his meaning. His words were garbled and strange. She kept trying to tell him, "No, I don't understand what you're saying."

Then she was running through a hallway, or a set of hallways. He was ahead of her.

"You have to keep going," he was saying. "Don't stop."

"I'm not going to stop," she was saying back. "I promise I won't ever stop."

"You have to stay alive," he said. "That's the only way you can keep writing."

"I promise," she said. "I promise."

Suddenly he was in front of her in all of his awful glory. His pinky was out, pinky-swear style.

"Promise me," he said. "That you'll stay alive."

"I promise," she said again. "I promise."

He was the only thing that had kept her alive for so long. She owed him everything. How do you thank a person for that?

You don't. You can't. She realized that immediately.

He had said something to her that night when they had decided to go on their rampage. They had been sloppy drunk, falling over each other, laughing at jokes that no longer made sense.

"Kill your heroes," he had said.

"I'm trying," she told him in the dream, tossing and turning. "I'm trying."

The Grace That Comes by Violence

LORRIE CALLED IT "The Lost Weekend." Roger called it "The Last Weekend." Annabel was pregnant, so she wasn't drinking. Designated driver, everyone said. Lou didn't say anything at all.

They met on a Friday at a bar none of them had been to before. It was a dive. Roger was getting married a week from Tuesday. He had a reckless, harried look about him, as if he wasn't sure if he was signing his life away or making the best decision of his life. Roger had always been like that—impulsive, sharky. It was these qualities that drew the others to him, made them gather around him like moths to a flame. He wasn't the leader of the group—no, that was Lou—but he was the glue that kept them all together, or at least he had been when they had all been friends. They weren't friends anymore. Now they were strangers, fifteen years out of college, unsure how to behave around each other.

"How far along are you?" Lorrie asked Annabel.

"Five months."

"A boy or a girl?"

"We're waiting to see." Annabel instinctively put a hand on her stomach, as if protecting the baby who she hadn't met yet.

Conversation was stilted. Lou tapped his class ring on the table several times. They had all agreed to meet, one last hurrah before their old classmate got married and settled down, a sort of symbolic goodbye to their youth, even though most of them had been adults in their own right for years now. It was only Lou, who still went to punk shows and did cocaine on the weekends, who existed in a sort of extended childhood, Lou who they depended on to make this trip into any kind of adventure. Because it was adventure that they all wanted, adventure they craved, any kind of shakeup from the mundane middle-thirties lives they were all leading now.

Lorrie now lived in New Jersey, with her girlfriend. She commuted into the city to work in advertising. She had not been gay in college, and this new development surprised everyone. No one knew how to act around her; although it was a small change, it put everyone ill at ease. Advertising, too, was a shock. In college she had been the wildest of all of them, a performance artist, prone to lighting fires and staging protests against the fascist art department, which she claimed was stifling her creativity. Now she sat at the table drinking white wine, wearing a blazer and jeans, demure with a new short haircut that confused everyone.

Roger had come uptown from the financial district where he did something with high-frequency trading that the others pretended to understand. They had always known he was going to make a lot of money; he was a whiz with numbers when they had been in school together. He showed them pictures of his fiancée, who was tiny and blond and smiley. Roger and Annabel had dated in college, but they broke up when she had moved to Michigan for graduate school, and they were awkward with each other now, unsure and careful. They had exchanged a few emails over the years and Christmas cards, but nothing concrete.

If he was honest with himself, and he never was, Roger thought she looked good, even pregnant. She had that glow about her. He couldn't help but imagine what would have happened if she hadn't moved away. Would it be his baby instead of her new husband's? He pushed these thoughts away with a sip of his Miller High Life. It was no use thinking about the past. He had to focus on the present, on the Annabel who was sitting in front of him.

Annabel had pursued a PhD in English literature and now taught at a small community college in the Bronx. She was married. She rarely spoke of her husband, except that he was also a writer, and they were very happy. She seemed happy too, at ease in her own skin and at ease with the pregnancy, wise in that way that pregnant women often are. She could feel Roger's eyes on her, but she avoided his gaze. She too had thought, "what if," but she also knew that these thoughts were useless. Things had gone the way they had gone. There was no changing the past.

Lou was the most uncomfortable of the bunch. He worked as a music producer these days, made good money, and had a lot of fun spending it. He had no use for people who didn't share his freewheeling attitude. Already he could tell this weekend was going poorly. His old friends were stiff. They weren't the people he remembered; Roger who used to hitch his skateboard to the back of passing trucks and ride them around the city; Annabel who could drink grown men under the table; Lorrie who had slept with half the dorm. Who were these sedated, normal people? What had happened?

"All right," Lou said, hoping to break the tension. "Let's do shots."

The rapid consumption of alcohol did little to diffuse the awkwardness that had settled over them like soot. They clustered around the pool table, nursing drinks, while Lou kicked their asses, methodically and with relish.

"Do you remember that pool bar we used to go to?" Roger said. "Right by campus?"

"Do you think it's still there?" Lorrie asked. She flipped some of her bangs out of her face.

"It's not," Lou said. "They turned it into a McDonald's."

"Oh, that's a shame."

"Well, it has been fifteen years."

They all let that fact sink in for a moment. Lou was lining up his shot, and he took it in the interim, balls cracking. He looked the youngest of the four of them, his face unlined and sweet looking, framed by shoulder-length dark hair.

"Fifteen years, and I can still beat you at pool," Lou said.

"You always were the pool shark," Roger said.

"And the card shark, and the best at all the drinking games," Annabel offered. She felt uncomfortable not drinking, but she was doing her best to keep up with the conversation. "Face it. Lou is better than us at everything."

"I suppose you're right," Roger said. "We should just give up now and go home."

Lou flinched. "We have the whole weekend," he said, surprising himself at how much he wanted his old friends to stay. "Stay for another drink."

"Relax," Roger said. "I'm not going anywhere."

Annabel said she had to pee. Walked away.

Lorrie ordered another drink at the bar, a High Life. She was drunk, wobbling in her sensible two-inch heels, and she couldn't remember why she had thought this trip was a good idea. They had all taken hotel rooms at a hotel downtown, adjoining rooms, the girls in one room and the boys in another. Lorrie wondered if they would even make it back to their rooms tonight. She wanted nothing more than to go home to her partner, snuggle in bed, and watch *America's Next Top Model.*

"Why do you look so sad?" Lou asked Lorrie, breaking her out of her reverie.

"I'm just tired. Long day at work."

"We've all had long days," Roger said. He went to take his shot, missed, and uttered an expletive. "Lou, do you have any drugs on you, by any chance?"

"Roger, you're thirty-six. You do not need any fucking drugs," Lorrie admonished him.

Lou smiled a sly smile. He patted his shirt pocket. "Roger, my man."

A few minutes later, the three of them were crushed into the cramped bar bathroom while Lou scooped out bumps of cocaine with a set of keys. Lorrie hated herself for being roped into this. The coke made her feet sharper, but it also made her feel as if her teeth were going to break.

They reappeared from the bathroom to a furious Annabel. "I thought you all had left me," she said. "I swear, I step away for five minutes, and you disappear on me."

"We just went, uh, to take care of a few things. Nothing you need to worry about."

"Just because I'm pregnant doesn't mean I'm stupid," she said. "I know what you were all doing in there. I used to do it too, you know."

"All right, all right, super detective over here." Lou patted her on the back. He had a glassy smile on his face. "Come on now. Don't be mad."

"I'm not mad," she said, but she was. She sat at the table and said nothing for ten or fifteen minutes, while they resumed their game of pool and tried to act more sober than they were.

Roger was the first to say it. "This scene is played out. We need to move on."

"I know a nice place a few blocks from here," Lou said. "Live music. Who wants to do a little dancing?"

Annabel perked up. "What kind of dancing?"

"The best kind."

"Ew," Lorrie said.

"Okay, not that kind." Lou gathered up his leather jacket. "Come on. Let's go."

They spilled out into the autumn night like an egg breaking open. Lou led the charge, his nose red and running. They walked briskly, Annabel trailing behind. People surged around them, the Lower East Side on a Friday night, snatches of conversation burbling past. The sky was dark and huge. Finally they got to an unmarked red door, which Lou opened with a flourish. A large man stood in the doorway and nodded as Lou ushered them through.

"What is this place?" Annabel asked.

"Don't you worry your pretty little head about that," Lou said.

Inside, the walls were clutching and close. There were people everywhere: people spilling out of rooms in every direction, people at the bar, people by the stage. The music was deafening. Annabel held onto her purse. It was so loud that it was pure noise, guitar sounds and bass unintelligible, drum beats humming in all of their sternums, people slamming into them from all angles. Roger yelled something in Annabel's ear, but she couldn't hear him over the band. He grabbed her hand, and suddenly they were dancing, or something approximate to dancing, and Lorrie was throwing her hands up into the air, and Lou was grinning a skullcap grin, and they were all lost in the madness, and there was nothing to do but let go.

They pulsed with the music for a bit, letting themselves be wrapped up in it, falling apart and letting themselves be put back together again, their minds beautifully blank with sound. Lorrie was kicked in the ankle, but she didn't care; it had been so long since she had danced like this, so free and absolute, so pure, so at peace with herself. Roger was edgy from the coke, but he didn't mind; it felt right to be moving his body and holding Annabel's hand. He felt like a kid again. Annabel knew she shouldn't be here, but she held tight to Roger's fingers and tried to make space for herself in the crowd, her mind spinning, losing herself in the music.

She shouted at Roger. "Are you having a good time yet?"

"Yes!" he shouted back at her. "Are you?"

"I think so!"

"Good!"

They had lost Lou, lost him to the madness, and then suddenly he reappeared again, sporting three beers—one for him, one for each of them, except Annabel—and told them to follow him. They crushed their way through the crowd and followed him into a small room off the main stage where they could still hear the music, but now they could also hear themselves think.

"So," he said. "What do you think of this place?"

"It's amazing," Lorrie said. "How did you find it?"

"One of the kids I manage plays here sometimes."

It was just one example of the ways Lou was still plugged in and they were not. Annabel sat down in one of the red plush chairs in the small room, her feet aching. The rest of them followed suit.

"What's this band called?"

"I have no idea," Lou said. "But they're pretty great, aren't they?"

Annabel nodded. Lou had always been this way—inscrutable, cool, on a separate level than the rest of them. They had always depended on him for their kicks. It amazed her that fifteen years later, almost nothing had changed. They were along for the ride, no matter what strides any of them had made in their lives since college.

"Do you remember that show we went to at the Mercury Lounge, where Lou got into that fight with the bouncer?" Lorrie said.

"Oh, yeah," Roger said. "He wouldn't accept your fake ID, and you punched him in the face."

"It was not a fake ID," Lou said. "It was my real ID. I had just gotten a haircut. I tried telling him it was really me, and he didn't believe me." Lou rummaged around in his pocket and pulled out an ID card. "Look. It really doesn't look like me."

They clustered around him to look. Annabel got so close she could smell Lou—cigarettes, leather—and was surprised that after all these years, he still smelled the same. She remembered the last time they had been so close. The last night before graduation. Blushing, she pushed the memory away and moved away from Lou. It was no use to dredge up the past, not with Roger, and not with Lou. It would only lead to hurt feelings and bad memories. She didn't want to hurt Roger most of all—and he had the most to lose from all of this.

She still felt guilty, all these years later. She put a hand on her stomach. She had a new life now, she reminded herself. Her husband didn't even know about what had happened. She had never told anyone—not Lorrie, not her best friends back home. She had never breathed a word of it. Now the secret burned in her mouth like a star. She would never tell, she promised herself. Not when the truth could hurt so many people.

"Do you remember," Roger was saying, "when we all stole those shopping carts and rode them down Fourteenth

Street?" Annabel laughed a little too loudly. Lorrie took a sip of her drink, gesturing wildly with her hands.

"And we all crashed into that police car, and they were going to arrest us, but Lou talked them out of it?"

"I thought you were going to die in that thing," Annabel said. "I still have a scar on my elbow from falling out of it." She rolled up her sleeve to show the group. There was a crescent moon–shaped scar on her elbow, shiny and white.

"Whose idea was that?" Roger said.

"Lou's, of course."

"Lou is always the one with the ideas."

They all looked at Lou. What next? they seemed to be asking him.

"Well," he said. "What are you guys in the mood for?"

Annabel was afraid as she followed Lou into the abyss of the subway, Lorrie behind her, Roger bringing up the rear. She didn't know where he was leading them, and she wasn't sure she wanted to know. They took the L train into Williamsburg, silent the whole time, except for Roger's ruminations on college memories that none of them could place or remember. "Do you remember when—" he would start off, and one of them would say, "No, I don't," and he would be quiet for a while, and then start again. Annabel wished he would shut up.

They had met in an Earth science seminar. She had thought he was cute, sitting in the front row with his notebook and his pen and his textbook all in a line in front of him, and she had gathered the courage to ask him out over a series of weeks. They had gone to a party together. She had kissed him in front of the punch bowl. They had casually and then seriously dated all through college, the kind of power couple that other people despised for how happy they were.

She remembered, dimly, how happy she had been in those days. How naïve. She had imagined a whole life in front of her, a life with Roger. Babies and white picket fences and the whole thing. Now she had that, a house in upstate New York and a job at a community college in the Bronx that she commuted to a few times a week and a husband who loved her and a dog named Goldie and a baby on the way. And talk of more babies. A house full of babies, her husband liked to say as he rubbed her stomach in the evenings.

"I'm not a dog," she told him. "I'm not going to have a litter." But it was a nice thought.

Roger was a thing of the past. But she had to admit he looked good, with his new haircut, which had to be expensive, and his shirt sleeves rolled up around his tan forearms. She wondered how she looked to him, five months pregnant with someone else's child, with swollen ankles and a puffy face.

He never talked about his fiancée, she noticed. He never mentioned her. He was inscrutable to her now, a mysterious presence. She still remembered when she had been able to predict his every thought before he had it, when she had known all of his facial expressions and been able to catalogue them. This new Roger, this new person, however good he looked, was a stranger to her. She remembered waking up next to him in the tiny dorm twin beds, rolling over and seeing his face next to hers countless times. It was his same face, but now that face was connected to a person she didn't know at all.

"This is our stop," Lou said.

Annabel stood. It wasn't productive to have thoughts like this, she told herself. Just focus on the present.

They got off the train, and immediately Annabel was even more worried. They were in a desolate part of East Williamsburg, full of pickle warehouses and abandoned buildings. The smell of cooked pasta floated through the air. Graffiti covered every available surface. She walked quickly behind Lou, who seemed to know exactly where he was going. He took them down some side streets, where there was no one on the sidewalk, and down an alleyway.

"Where are we going?" Lorrie asked. She seemed even more apprehensive than Annabel felt, her sensible heels tapping the ground in nervousness. Annabel remembered that Lorrie had once been the one who was down for anything, who would go to any party, no matter what time of night it was. She would jump on any harebrained scheme, no matter how far-fetched it was. This new Lorrie wore blazers and had a three hundred dollar haircut. She couldn't imagine this new Lorrie doing lines of molly off of a toilet seat in their dormitory and then traveling to Astoria to go to an underground rave in a parking lot behind a Wendy's drive-through.

"Don't worry about it," Lou said. He finally stopped at the side of an abandoned-looking building and knocked twice on the door.

There were sounds of music from inside, loud music. Another underground rave? Annabel thought to herself.

She wasn't prepared for that. The club had been enough for her; now she just wanted to go back to her hotel room and lie down. The door swung open, and an enormous tattooed man answered.

"Louis."

"Mac."

"I thought Andy said you weren't welcome here anymore."

"We, uh, we had a little chat." Lou rocked from heel to heel. "We're good now, I promise."

"You sure about this? Who're your friends?"

"They're cool." Lou nodded his head in Roger and Lorrie's direction. About Annabel, he said nothing. Annabel wondered how she must look—a pregnant woman, trying to gain entrance into whatever illicit activity this was. She smiled up at Mac, trying to gain favor. He glowered down at her, dubious.

"Behave yourself," he said, and it seemed as if he were speaking only to Annabel.

They walked through the doorway, down a long hallway, and into a huge open room. There was a cluster of men inside in a loose circle. In the middle of the circle, two men were fighting, bare chests and bare fists. The men were slick with blood and sweat. The men around them cheered and shouted, egging them on.

Annabel's mouth fell open. "Lou," she said. "What did you bring us into?"

"This," Lou said. "This is a good time."

*

Roger had never seen two men fight like this before. He had never seen a fight before. He had grown up in suburban New Jersey, and he had never gotten into a bar fight, never slapped anyone. His whole life had been nonviolent. He didn't believe in violence. He had dabbled in vegetarianism in college. He gave money to PETA.

But something about it, something about watching them go at it, triggered some mechanism within him. It lit a fire in his belly. He found himself cheering along with the crowd as one of the men, a slight, towheaded man with eyes like chips of ice, threw a punch like a sledgehammer into the other man's stomach. The man dropped like a ton of bricks. But he was already up again and sprinting toward his opponent, and suburban Roger was yelling along with the crowd as they collided again, blood flying through the air. Lou was beside him, his best friend, united by violence. Roger threw an arm around Lou's shoulders, and Lou left it there. Previously, they had been so uncomfortable with each other that such a gesture would not be tolerated. But now the boundaries had melted, and they were as they had always been, two brothers in arms, united by the fight.

Lorrie gasped. The fighters were bloody, they were panting, and yet they excited something in her too, something primal. She wanted to see how it would end. Only Annabel was truly horrified, couldn't look, but also couldn't look away, as the two men beat each other up in the center of the circle. Lou presented them with a bottle of whiskey that no one remembered him buying, and they—minus Annabel—took turns swigging from it. They did bumps of cocaine out in the open. There was no one to stop them. There were worse things going on in this crowd around them.

The crowd surged and moved along with the fight, which melted and changed as the men moved around. Annabel couldn't stop watching. She had never seen such a thing. The blond fighter was skillful and sharp, sending cutting shots into the darker fighter's ribs and torso. But the darker fighter had an endurance about him; he took the shots like a truck, barely hesitating before he fired back at his opponent. They sprung apart, circling each other, and then snapped together again for a flurry of activity, then were flung apart again. The crowd cheered when one of them went down and cheered even louder when someone got up again.

"They're waiting for a knockout," Lou said, looking at Annabel. "They're waiting for one of them to go down for good."

"Are there rounds, like boxing?" Annabel wracked her brain for fighting knowledge and came up mostly empty.

"No, it's not like that. Hang on." Lou disappeared into the crowd and reappeared a few minutes later, holding a piece of paper. "I just put some money down on the blond fighter. He's a monster. I've seen him fight before. The other guy is just some guy they found because no one wants to fight the blond guy."

"You're gambling?"

"Relax. It's just a harmless bet."

"Are you sure?"

"I do it all the time," he said. "I've even made some money."

She turned her eyes away from Lou and looked at the men fighting in the middle of the circle. The blond fighter was pummeling the smaller man. She didn't enjoy displays of violence. Roger was enraptured, she noticed. Lou couldn't stop cheering. Why were men so interested in fighting? She thought their energy could be spent elsewhere.

"Uh, Lou, where's the bathroom?" Annabel asked. She had been holding in this question for too long, and now it had become urgent.

"Here, I'll show you."

He walked her around the perimeter of the warehouse, ignoring the shouting of the men and the various drunken stumblers who tried to intercept them. "I'm happy for you," he said gruffly, not looking at her, in a way that made her think he wasn't happy for her at all.

"Thank you. I'm excited." She smiled at him, but he didn't return the expression.

"I know this is what you always wanted."

Annabel's face flickered, confused. She had never thought that this was what she had wanted until it had already happened.

"Are you serious?" she said. "I never said that."

"I know," he said. "But you know. You were always the one who took care of all of us."

"I don't know about that."

"I'm just saying. You'll be a good mother."

"You would have been a good father too."

Lou laughed, a short barking sound. "Right."

"I always thought so."

"Don't flatter me," he said. "You're no good at it."

Annabel felt her throat lock up. There were so many things she could have said, and she didn't know how to say any of them.

They reached the bathroom door. He ushered her through it. She wished there was something she could say to make this better, but there was nothing. She looked at his face—the same as it always had been, Lou's lovely open face—and found no answers.

"Go on," he said.

So she did.

The two men were still going at it when she got back. She wiped her wet hands on the sides of her pants and searched Lou's face for signs of something—anything. She found nothing. He was fixated on the fight, on making his money. Roger was elated next to him, cheering and taking swigs from the whiskey bottle, and Annabel felt sick to her stomach. She looked to Lorrie for some signal, some companionship, but Lorrie was as still and silent as a stone, her face unreadable.

"He's going to win the bet," she said to Lorrie.

"I know," Lorrie said. "Then we'll have some money to spend this weekend."

The two men were circling each other, panting, the darker fighter bleeding profusely from a cut on his forehead. He was clearly faltering, his knees bent into a catlike position, ducking punches that seemed to come faster and faster.

Then, suddenly, as if inspired by some grace of God, he threw a wild punch at the blond fighter. It was a knock-out punch. The blond fighter spun, fell, and crashed to the ground.

The crowd erupted into cheers, most of them negative. The blond fighter's corner man ventured into the center of the circle to pick him up. He was bleeding from his mouth and nose, and there were bruises all over his bare chest and torso.

Lou's face turned white in a way that Annabel had never seen before.

"We need to go," he said. "We need to go, now."

"Why?" Roger said. "The fun is just starting."

"I'll explain later," Lou said. "Just follow me."

They slipped out the back of the building. Lou led them down a side street, stopping to light a cigarette, and they walked quickly down Bushwick Avenue, Lou looking over his shoulder the whole time. They crossed onto a side street and kept walking, faster than was comfortable for Annabel, until they got to a bar that she didn't recognize. Lou ushered them inside, ordered four drinks, seeming to forget that Annabel wasn't drinking. He sat them all down at a four-top table in the back and said some words to the bartender that Annabel didn't hear.

Lorrie looked confused. Roger looked disappointed. Lou looked positively terrified.

He drank half of his beer in one gulp, then slammed the glass onto the table. He didn't say anything. Lorrie was the one who spoke up finally.

"Lou," she said. "What the hell just happened?"

Annabel was reminded of a time when they had been in college, and Lou had started a fire in his dorm room, trying to burn photographs of an ex-girlfriend none of them had liked. The RA had smelled smoke and came knocking on the door, but the fire was already out of control, and the fire department had to be called to put out the blaze. Lou was almost kicked out of the dorm and was allowed to stay only because he claimed he had no knowledge of how the fire started.

Now he had the same guilty look on his face, the same shame, the same fear, as he had when he talked to that RA. The same acknowledgment that he had somehow irreparably fucked up.

What had he done? Annabel wondered. That fight club was obviously illegal, and he had obviously lost his bet. But it seemed to be more than that. It seemed to be dangerous. She had never seen him scared like this. His face and knuckles were white. His hands were shaking. His eyes flitted back and forth like a skittish dog's. He kept looking at the door of the bar, as if he was afraid that someone was going to come in and bust him. But who?

"I've made some bad bets lately," Lou said finally. "A lot of bad bets, actually. With money that isn't mine."

"What do you mean, with money that isn't yours?"

"I've been borrowing money," he explained carefully. "From a man. You don't need to know his name. In fact, it's better if you don't know his name at all. I've been making these bets, and I've lost a lot of money."

"What does that have to do with us?" Lorrie asked.

She had always had the determination of a bull terrier to find the truth, Annabel remembered suddenly. You could never lie to Lorrie. You could never tell her, no, I feel sick, I'm not coming out tonight. She would show up at your dorm room with a bottle of Jose Cuervo and a bowl of chicken soup, and that would be that.

"It doesn't have anything to do with you, except that you're with me," Lou said. "So you're a part of it now too. These men are going to come looking for me eventually, and as long as you're with me, they'll come looking for you too."

"So why are we still with you?"

"We can't just abandon him if he's going to get killed," Roger said. "Besides. It's the Last Weekend."

"I'm not going to get killed," Lou said. "Just beaten up a little bit, most likely. I think. I wasn't even supposed to be at that fight. I've been kicked out of that ring for betting before. I already owe the owners money."

"Why did you bring us there then?"

"You said you wanted a good time."

"You risked your life to show us a good time?" Lorrie asked.

"What can I say?" Lou said. "I'm a great friend."

"I think we should split up," Lorrie said. "Lou, you should go somewhere. Somewhere they can't find you."

"They know where I live. They know where I hang out. I only brought you all to this bar because it's the last place they'd look for me. My ex-girlfriend is the bartender." He gestured with his hand. The bartender waved at them. "So they'll assume I'd never set foot in here."

"We can't split up now," Roger said. "It's only Friday night. This is supposed to be my bachelor's weekend, isn't it? We can't let a little violence spoil the party."

Annabel looked at Roger in shock. She didn't recognize him, this man who had been so gentle when she had known him. He had never even been in a fight. Who was Roger now? This hard-partying, gun-slinging person. Was getting married changing him this much? She was afraid to find out.

"That's very sweet of you," Lou was saying. "But this is my mess. I need to clean it up on my own. I can borrow some money from a guy in Chinatown. Pay off my debt. It'll just get me deeper in the hole, but it'll keep the monkey off my back for now."

"So we'll go with you," Roger said. "Come on. We're all best friends, right? This is what we do. We help each other."

"I guess Roger's right," Lorrie said. "Besides. How hard can it be? To go see a man and borrow some money?"

"It's too late at night to go now. We can go in the morning." Lou drained his drink. "We should all go back to the hotel now. They won't find us there."

"Call a car." Lorrie put her hand over Lou's. "It's going to be okay. I promise."

That was just like Lorrie. To make a promise with no understanding of whether it could be kept. But it made Lou feel just a tiny bit better that he had gotten his friends into this mess, and he smiled at his old friend. It would be okay, he thought to himself. He just had to get the money and pay his debt, and they wouldn't break his kneecaps.

It was so simple. So simple, it couldn't possibly go wrong.

*

The ride to the hotel was an hour, but it was almost completely silent. They said goodnight and went their separate ways. Annabel was exhausted, but she didn't know if she would be able to sleep. She lay in bed for a while with the lights off, listening to Lorrie's steady breathing, before she got out of bed and walked quietly to the hotel's roof deck, which strangely wasn't closed off yet. She stood on the deck and looked out at the city, which looked like someone had taken a jar of fireflies and shaken it up. It was beautiful up there at night, with the sounds of traffic rushing below her. She lived upstate now and taught in the Bronx, so rarely did she get to see Manhattan in all its glory, and she smiled to see its beauty was still intact.

"Couldn't sleep?" a familiar voice sounded behind her.

It was Roger. He was the last person she expected to see out here and also the last person she wanted to see. She was still shaken up by his reaction to the fight—so different from the person she had known in college. She kept looking for signs of the old Roger, but he had been eclipsed by this new person, this high-powered finance official who liked to watch men beat each other up and was getting married in a week and didn't love her anymore. Did he? She couldn't tell. She supposed a part of her would always love him, and she had come to terms with that fact a long time ago. When she left for graduate school, she had let him go, but she realized now that a part of her had been holding on to the what-if of their relationship for all this time. Now she was seeing that it was gone.

"No. You?"

"I can never sleep in hotels. They're too sterile."

Roger lit a cigarette—another new habit he seemed to have picked up—and came to stand next to her. "Wow. The city is beautiful at night."

It was such a simple statement; of course, the city *was* beautiful at night, but it struck Annabel. Roger was still capable of recognizing beauty. Her Roger, he was still in there somewhere.

"Yes," she said. "It is."

"You should be sleeping," he said. "You're growing a person. You need to get your rest."

It was his first direct reference to her pregnancy, which somehow she had forgotten about. In just a few moments, she had reverted back to her college self, and she was simply a girl standing on a rooftop with a boy she liked. But then the spell was over, and she was married and pregnant again, and she had to act like it.

"One night of bad sleep won't kill me," she said. "I'll make it up somehow."

"What does it feel like?" he said. "Being pregnant, I mean?"

"I don't know," she said. "It's hard to describe." She didn't know how to describe it to Roger, of all people. She didn't know how to talk to him. "It's a good feeling though. Once you get over all the morning sickness and the feeling heavy and the nerves."

"It looks good on you. You look at peace."

"Thank you."

They stood in silence for a while, Roger smoking. He stood downwind from her so he wasn't blowing smoke directly at her.

"I can't believe I'm getting married," he said. "You know, I always thought I'd only get married to you. For years, you know. After."

"I know," she said, surprising herself with the quickness of her answer. "I thought that too. For a long time."

"But you met someone. And I met someone."

"We did."

"It's just such an odd thing, you know?"

"I know."

"People change, I guess."

She wanted to say so many things, but she didn't know how to say any of them. I didn't change, she wanted to say. *I've always loved you. I always will.* But none of those things were appropriate, none of them would have changed anything, the chips had fallen, and they were separated forever by time and distance and the forces of other people. There was no way to change the past. If she had never seen Roger again, she could have lived her life and been perfectly happy, but now that she had seen him, she realized all the things she had given up, all the things she had lost, and her Roger was gone, replaced by this person who said such awful things, and at the same time, he looked like and moved like her Roger, and before she knew what she was doing, she was closing the distance between them.

"I didn't change," she whispered into his mouth. And then they were kissing, kissing like they always had, and it felt familiar and alien at the same time. He was working his hand into the waistband of her pants, and she was looking for blind spots on the video cameras.

*

When Annabel had left for graduate school, she and Roger had talked about staying together. They had talked about long distance. "It's only five years," she had said. But that "only" had hung in the air between them like a curse. It was too long to be separated, to live lives that weren't in direct conjunction with each other. "We'll visit, we'll talk, we'll call," he had said. But they hadn't done any of those things. They had let each other drift. Now, it seemed, after fifteen years, they were finding their way back to each other. It felt familiar, easy, simple, like two puzzle pieces locking back together. Annabel felt no guilt. When they snuck back into their hotel rooms that night, they kissed for the last time. She knew she would not leave her husband for him, but it was a nice feeling at the same time, a moment of closure, as if she needed to get Roger out of her system once and for all. Prove that what had happened between them was real, that it had happened. That he still felt something for her, and she for him.

She didn't know if that was how he felt—she was afraid to ask. She had a sinking feeling that he would drop everything for her, that he would leave his fiancée and start a new life with her, but she didn't want to bring it up. This was the end, she told herself. It ended here. Just two old friends, revisiting something that had ended a long time ago. She slipped into her room and tried to fall asleep. She was awake for several more hours before she finally slept. When she dreamed, it was of the new baby, of the future, not of the past.

*

In the morning, Roger was subtly attentive. He opened doors for her, pulled her chair out in the dining room where they had their continental breakfast. Lou and Lorrie noticed but said nothing. They were used to Annabel and Roger being in their own world, and there was nothing they could say or do to take them out of it. Lou was on edge anyway, nervous and frustrated, and he didn't say much, just picked dejectedly at his food. Lorrie tried valiantly to make conversation, but without the lubrication of alcohol, there was little to talk about. They were four strangers again, back at square one.

They set out to see the man in Chinatown around noon. Lou was nervy, jumpy like a racehorse. He smoked several cigarettes on the walk to the subway, tapped his foot on the whole train ride, made ignorant small talk. Annabel and Roger were in their own little world and ignored everyone else. Lorrie amused herself with her phone. She missed her partner and wanted desperately for this whole affair to be over so she could go home. She had a hangover from the night before and had tried to kill it by drinking whiskey in her coffee, but it wasn't enough; she still felt terrible. She was tired of her friends, although she wouldn't have admitted it. She was trying to remember what had brought them together in the first place. She no longer had anything in common with these people, nothing but shared history. And it wasn't enough.

Chinatown was bustling. People surged back and forth on the narrow streets. Lou seemed to know where they were going, and they ducked around people selling touristy merchandise and vendors hocking fruit on side streets. People yelled things at them in Chinese. Bike messengers flew by. Neon signs displayed all sorts of Chinese characters. Lou led them down an alleyway to a blue door, where he rang the doorbell twice and the door opened. They walked up three flights of narrow stairs.

At the top of the stairs was a large room where a small Chinese man sat at a desk.

"Louis," the man said without looking up from a pile of papers. "I was wondering when I would see you again."

"Mr. Mark," Lou said. "It's good to see you."

"It's never good to see me," the man said. "Don't lie. It's unbecoming."

"So you know why I'm here."

"I was told you'd be coming."

"You were?" Lou looked scared. "By who?"

A large man stepped out from a door to the right of the desk. Annabel recognized him as the doorman from the fight club. He was enormous, heavily tattooed on both arms, and he kept cracking his knuckles. Another man followed him, holding a baseball bat.

"Lou," the first man said. "We thought you'd come here."

"I guess I'm more predictable than I thought," Lou said. Annabel could tell he was trying to keep the fear out of his voice. "Now, can you let me borrow some money so I can pay you nice gentlemen?"

"It's not going to work like that," the Chinese man said. "You already owe me more than you can pay, and they have to give you some incentive to pay it back."

"Come on, guys. Just this once. I've been a good customer. You know I'm good for it."

"We don't know that, actually."

"Please," Lou said. "Come on. Please."

"Don't worry," the Chinese man said. "They won't do any real damage. Nothing permanent."

The larger man advanced. Before Annabel knew what was happening, Lou was flying backwards into the wall, blood gushing from his nose. The man with the baseball bat hung back, possibly waiting to see what would happen next. Lou fell to the ground. The large man delivered a series of vicious kicks to Lou's ribs and stomach, and Lou cried out. He reached out, trying to defend himself, but the large man was too strong, and Lou was already on the ground, prone and defenseless. The whole encounter lasted less than a minute, and then the man was stepping back, leaving Lou lying on the floor, bleeding.

"Next time," the larger man said, "we won't be so forgiving."

"You call this forgiving?" Lou spat, blood pooling from his lips.

"We're letting you keep all your parts. Now get out of here. And take your friends with you."

Roger bent down and helped Lou to his feet. "We've got to get him to a hospital," he said. "I'm sure he has broken ribs."

"There's no point," Lou said. "They'll just tape them up and send me home. Take me to my apartment. I can tape my own ribs there. I don't have insurance anyhow."

They limped down the stairs. Out on the street, there was some confusion over what to do. Lou was in a lot of pain; Annabel could tell by his shallow breathing. His nose and mouth were bleeding.

"Call a car, we'll go to your apartment," she said. "We can't take him back to the hotel."

"Why not?" Lorrie said.

"He'll get blood everywhere," Roger said. "We'll have to clean it up."

"I just want to go home," Lou said. "I'll call a car."

They called a car and piled in when it came. Annabel held Lou's hand the whole ride, letting him squeeze it when they went over potholes. His building was a walk-up, and they struggled to get Lou up the stairs.

Lou's apartment was spartan. Annabel had expected a mess, but he had very few possessions. A television set, a leather couch, a bed that had recently been made. A few cooking implements. The walls were painted red. They got Lou to the bed and laid him down, gave him some Oxy-Contin they had found in his medicine cabinet (leftover from when he had had his wisdom teeth removed, he said—Annabel didn't know if she believed him) and waited until he drifted off to sleep. There was some talk about whether they should stay, wait and see if those men were going to come back, but none of them wanted to wait around in that case. They felt strange, leaving Lou unprotected and injured in his apartment alone, so it was finally decided that they would sleep in shifts on the couch, drinking Lou's whiskey and waiting around for him to wake up and get well enough that he could take care of himself.

They ordered takeout and spent the evening playing cards and eating bad Chinese food. It felt familiar. They were getting used to each other again, getting used to each other's habits and tics, working out the kinks of being separated for so long. Annabel almost had the sense that after this, they would keep in touch again. She had missed this—the camaraderie, the engagement, the friendship.

They all fell asleep on the couch—so much for shifts—and slumped against one another, like how they used to sleep in each other's dorm rooms, crushed into twin beds. Annabel remembered, dimly, as she was falling asleep, how she used to know her friends' bodies better than she knew her own. It felt good to be here with all of them once again. It felt right. She had good dreams.

Annabel was awoken in the middle of the night by a sound coming from the small kitchenette attached to the living room. There was movement at the kitchen counter. She got up and made her way over to the kitchen to find Lou pouring himself a glass of water.

"Jesus," she said. "You scared me."

In the dark, Lou's face glowed. "I'm sorry," he said. "Do you want some water?"

She took a sip from his glass. "So," he said. "You and the boy are back at it again, huh?"

"What?"

"You and Roger."

"I don't know," she said. "I guess so."

"That's cool." The way he said it was mean, nasty, like he definitely did not think it was cool at all. His breathing through the broken ribs was labored, and it seemed like every movement was causing him pain.

"It's fine, Lou."

"I'm sure it is," he said.

"You know, you could always make a different choice." Lou's eyebrows flagged.

"What? And choose you?" She said it too sharply and realized she sounded mean.

"I'm just saying."

"We slept together once." Annabel bit her lip. "It was just something that happened."

It had happened at the last party of the year. They had been drunk, both of them. Afterwards, they had been guilty and nervous around each other, unable to look each other in the eye. She had never told anyone. She would never tell anyone. It had been a mistake. Hadn't it? She had always thought so. But now Lou was making it seem as if they had a future together, as if that was something he wanted. Lou wasn't really a future type of guy.

"It was more than that," he said.

"What are you saying?"

"I think you know what I'm saying."

"Just say it."

"I'm saying I want you," he said slowly, measuring out his words. "I always have."

"Well, you've got a funny way of showing it."

He kissed her, a bumpy kiss that almost missed her mouth, an awkward kiss that felt more wrong than right. But she felt herself leaning into it all the same. Lou. Her best friend. His strange, feline way of being, his mysterious ways, his unreadable face. She had never been able to unlock him; now he was inviting her inside.

She pulled away after a beat too long. "Lou," she said. "I can't do this."

"You are doing it," he said. "Come on, Annabel."

"No," she said. "It's too confusing. Too complicated."

"You know that night meant something," he said. "You wouldn't have kissed me like that if it didn't."

"It might have meant something then, but that was fifteen years ago."

"And what? You'll get back together with Roger, but not with me?"

"Roger and I have a history. Something to fall back on."

"And you and I, we don't have history? I've loved you since I was eighteen years old."

"You never told me that. You never said—I didn't know. I didn't know any of that, Lou. You were always just my best friend. Someone good for laughs, for kicks."

"Is that all I am to you? Good for kicks?"

"No, of course not."

She couldn't see his facial expression in the dark, but she knew he was hurt.

"Look," she said. "You mean a lot to me. But it's too complicated, all of us together like this. Roger is the one. He always has been. And besides, I'm married now. It's not like I'm going to leave my husband and run off with one of you. It's just a weekend, a blip on the radar, and then we're all going to go back to our lives and pretend none of this ever happened."

"Is that so?" Lou said. "Maybe you should ask Roger how he feels about that."

"It doesn't matter how he feels about it. That's my decision, and that's what I'm going to do. It's impossible to change the past. This is what happened, and this is how it's going to go."

There was a noise from the other room. Roger appeared around the kitchen counter, rubbing his eyes. The light switch was flicked, and all three of them were suddenly thrown into brightness.

"What are you two doing up?" Roger said. "It's four in the morning."

"Ask him," Lou said. "Ask him if this meant anything. If any of it does."

"Lou, please."

"Or do you want me to tell him?"

"Lou, you're being cruel." Annabel felt sick to her stomach. "Please, stop this."

"Ask me what?" Roger said. He saw the two of them standing too close together. "Annabel, what's going on?"

"Annabel here told me that the two of you aren't getting back together. That this was a one-time thing. That she's just messing around on anyone, everyone."

"Lou!" Annabel said sharply. "You don't need to do this."

"And she didn't tell you, of course, about me and her."

"What about you and her? Annabel, what's going on?"

"Do you remember the last party of the year? The night before graduation? When you got too drunk and had to go home early?" Lou was on a roll now, meanness edging into his voice, momentum growing behind his words. "Annabel and I, we had a little party of our own that night. And she never told you, never told anyone apparently, not a word."

"Annabel," Roger said. "Is any of what he's saying true?"

"Roger," she said. "It wasn't like that. We were just kids. It was just something that happened."

"She was about to go off to school, and she thought there would be no consequences," Lou continued. "She's always had a thing for me, you know."

"That's not how it went," Annabel said. "We were really drunk, and I don't know how it happened."

That was a lie. She remembered exactly how it happened: Lou in his leather jacket, leaning over her, smelling of beer and cigarette smoke, so different from Roger who was always clean-shaven and smiling. Lou inviting her back to his room, promising her a drink, and her accepting the offer, knowing exactly what would happen. It hadn't been premeditated, but the subtext behind his words had been implicit. She had understood exactly what she was doing, and she had done it anyway, and it seemed that now she was paying the price.

"I can't believe this," Roger said. "You—you didn't. You never told me. You—how could you?"

"It was stupid. I was being stupid. I was scared, and I was leaving, and I didn't know what I was doing."

"And now, what? You two are rekindling whatever that was?"

"No," Annabel said. "No, of course not."

"Was that what this weekend was to you? Just an excuse to fuck around? Is that what I am to you? Just someone to use and throw away, a piece of history?"

"No, you're so much more than that. Roger, I loved you."

"Loved. Past tense."

"I'm married now. It's different."

"And I'm getting married. That didn't seem to stop you last night."

"Last night was a mistake. I wasn't thinking. I just—I missed you. Of course I missed you. It was just a habit."

"So I'm a habit now." Roger's face twisted into something nasty. "Right."

"No, of course not. You're my first love. You're my Roger. You're always going to have a place in my heart." She turned to Lou. "You both are."

Lou gritted his teeth. "Annabel," he said. "I think you should leave."

"It's four in the morning."

"I'll call you a car. Back to the hotel."

"But what about the Lost Weekend? The Last Weekend?" she said feebly, as if tradition would save her. She knew it was too late, the boys already hated her. She wished Lorrie were awake and here to defend her, but Lorrie had stayed fast asleep through the whole ordeal.

"It's Sunday," Lou said. "Consider the weekend officially over."

Roger and Lou watched Annabel leave with sinking feelings in their stomachs. She was going back to her husband, to her life.

Roger knew he had a fiancée to go home to, but he had never felt so alone in his life. He couldn't talk to his fiancée the way he had been able to talk to Annabel. He suddenly thought that he would never be able to talk to anyone again. He didn't want to look at Lou, the man who had tried to steal his girlfriend, so he grabbed his jacket and told him that he was going for a walk. He'd be back, he said, but Roger had no intention of returning. This whole weekend had been a nightmare. Running from thugs trying to beat Lou into a pulp, the underground fight, drinking more alcohol than he had consumed all year. Roger had a headache. He broke out into the night and started walking.

There were almost no people on the streets. Roger lit a cigarette from the pack he had taken from Lou's apartment. He didn't usually smoke, but he had picked up the habit over the weekend, and now he couldn't seem to kick it. His head was spinning. With rejection, with fear, with confusion. It all led back to Annabel, to the time they'd spent together in college when he had been on top of the world, the kind of guy people wanted to be friends with, the kind of guy people wanted to be. He had been popular, well liked, well respected. He had been one-half of a power couple that people envied. Now he had a high-powered job and a beautiful fiancée, but it didn't feel the same. He wasn't the same. He had lost something, something intangible. Maybe it was his confidence. He wasn't as cocky as he had been back then. He had gotten older. Life had knocked him back on his heels a few times. He knew what was lurking in the shadows.

He found himself walking over the Williamsburg Bridge. He was reminded of the night on the roof with Annabel, looking out over the city. Had that really only been last night? So much had happened since then. It had been a long weekend. He suddenly knew where he was heading—to the hotel, to find Annabel. He had to talk to her, one more time, before she was lost to him forever. He had to find her. It was his last chance. If he blew this, there was no chance that he would ever be happy again. He couldn't risk that. He needed—what? Closure. Some way to resolve the boiling in his blood.

He kept walking, dodging bike messengers and the few passersby who were still on the streets at this hour. He walked until the sun came up. It was just starting to get light out when he reached the hotel, went upstairs, and knocked on Annabel's door.

Lorrie woke up with a pounding headache and went into Lou's bedroom. He was asleep. She shook him lightly, and he groaned.

"Uh," he said. "What time is it?"

"Almost ten. I thought I'd make you some breakfast. Where are Roger and Annabel?"

"Annabel left. Roger said he was going for a walk, but I don't know if he's coming back."

"Why did Annabel leave?"

"It's complicated."

"Does it have to do with the fact that you slept with her on the night of our graduation party?"

"Who told you?"

"No one needed to tell me. I'm not an idiot. I could tell by the fact that you two wouldn't look at each other at graduation," Lorrie said.

Lou grimaced. It didn't help that his friend didn't miss a beat.

"Roger finally found out, huh? That you carry a torch for his girlfriend?"

"Yeah, something like that."

"If you love her, you should go after her."

"It's not going to work. I tried that. She doesn't love me." Lou rolled over and pulled the covers over his eyes. "I should just move on with my life. Besides, we didn't talk for fifteen years. How about we just forget about all this and don't talk for another fifteen?"

"We could try that," Lorrie said. "Or you could make a big romantic gesture."

"To a married woman?"

"You never know."

"Jesus," Lou said. "I hate it when you're smart."

"That's why they pay me the big bucks," Lorrie said. "Come on. I'll call you a car."

Annabel opened her hotel room door to find Roger, smelling of cigarettes, standing in her doorway.

"You shouldn't be here," she said. "I'm packing up my things. I'm going home."

"I want you to stay," he said. "I love you. I want you. I want you to stay with me."

"Roger, no. I have a life. I like my life. I'm not going to run away with you."

"Why not?"

"Because your idea of me is based on who I was when I was twenty-one. You don't really know me. I'm a different person now. I have a whole different life."

"Just do a trial run. Give me a week."

"I'm not giving you anything."

"Please," he said.

She threw some items in a suitcase, zipped it shut, and brushed by him into the hallway. "No."

"I promise I'll give you a good life," he said. "I can make you happy."

"I am happy," she said. "I'm very happy. I don't need anyone else to make me happy. I want to have this baby with my husband. I want to keep teaching my classes at the community college. I don't want anything to change."

"You're just scared," he said. "You were always the woman I thought I was going to end up with."

"You'd really do that?" she said. "You'd throw away your whole life, your whole relationship, just to be with me?"

"Yes," he said with certainty. "I would."

They were standing in the hallway of the hotel, and Annabel was acutely aware that they were making too much noise, that they were going to wake up other hotel guests. Then Lou rounded the corner, flowers in hand.

"Annabel, wait. Don't leave yet."

"What are you doing?" she said.

"I'm here to tell you something," Lou said. "I've always loved you. I want to be with you. I can't live without you. Please, forget about Roger. Choose me instead."

"It's not a choice," she said. "It's not like I'm choosing pie or cake for dessert. I can't believe the two of you are making me do this."

"You have to pick one of us," Roger said, sensing he had the upper hand. "You can only love one of us, right? So pick one." He stood next to Lou, shoulder to shoulder. "It can't be that difficult a choice."

Lou grinned at her, his typical lopsided Lou grin. Roger looked hopeful.

"I love both of you," Annabel said. "In different ways. I'm not doing this. I'm going home to my husband, who loves me. Who gave me this baby. That's what I'm doing, and that's my final decision."

She collected her suitcase and her purse and started walking down the hallway. The two men stood behind her, confused, angry, unsure of what to do next. They waited until she was in the elevator before Roger threw the first punch.

When security finally came to break them up, Roger was bleeding from his nose and mouth, Lou had broken another rib, and both of them were breathing heavily. They were tossed onto the curb and stared at each other for a while before Roger stuck out his hand.

"I forgive you," he said. "I know you didn't do it to hurt me."

"I forgive you," Lou said. "I know you were just trying to protect your interests."

"But maybe we should wait another fifteen years before we hang out again," Roger said.

"Agreed."

They hugged, slapped each other on the back, and separated. Roger stepped into a deli to get napkins to wipe the blood from his face, and that was the last Lou saw of him.

Lou walked into the subway, wincing heavily with every movement. His body ached terribly. The rocking of the subway lulled him to sleep.

Annabel was gone. Annabel was gone forever. The dream he had held onto for fifteen years, the vague possibility that one day she would wake up and realize she wanted him, it was over. He felt strangely relieved, as if he had been living under a huge weight for as long as he could remember. It truly was the Lost Weekend. He had been lost, and now he had found a part of himself that he had forgotten about. He would move on. He would be all right. He knew this, suddenly, as surely as he knew the earth was round. He was free of her. He would be okay.

Annabel took the Metro upstate and was picked up from the train station by her husband, who asked, "Honey, did you have a good time?"

"I had an interesting time," she said. "I saw some things I didn't expect to see."

Like the volatility of human beings, she thought but did not say. Like sheer ugliness. Like brutality.

Like the grace that comes by violence. She looked out the window at the neat suburban streets and imagined living with Roger in Manhattan in some high-rise building. She imagined living in Lou's seedy Bushwick apartment. There were so many threads, so many possibilities, and this was what she had chosen. She wondered if she had chosen incorrectly. But then her husband put his hand on her thigh, and she knew she hadn't. This was where she belonged—clean, safe streets where everything was predictable and she felt sure of herself. There were no fight clubs here, no dive bars, no thugs trying to beat her with a baseball bat. There was only love, a warm collision of sofa cushions, and falling asleep with the TV on.

Lou and Roger could have their fast-paced lives. She was here. She didn't want to take any more risks.

She chose love, in its purest form. Without violence.

The Most Normal Day
in Existence

THE PSYCHIATRIST, OUT of pocket, is four hundred dollars. Dolly walks, head held high, through his waiting room with stolen cigarettes in her purse, a compulsion she still can't shake despite years of trying. The stealing, not the smoking. The smoking is simply habit, like biting your nails, and she could stop if she wanted, but she doesn't bother. Too much work.

He gives her the bad news in two parts: *No, you won't ever feel much better. Take these pills.*

She observes him carefully. He's older, white, not unpleasant. He's not trying to victimize her. She has a man at home not unlike him, just a little younger, a little rougher around the edges. Lately, she's been domestic—cooking, cleaning the kitchen, trying to please him—although he barely notices. She smokes; he doesn't like it. But he smokes too, furtively, when he's drinking, which is always. Late at night, she catches him sneaking pulls from the whiskey bottle.

The psychiatrist looks at her. *Do you understand?*

"Yes," Dolly says. "I understand."

She doesn't know what he's just said. Diagnoses ring in her ears. She has just thrown away four hundred dollars. She takes the prescription slip from his sweaty palms. She walks out of the room. She is not crazy. She is a normal person with a job and a boyfriend and a life. She is normal.

It is only later, in the taxi back to Brooklyn, that she cries.

The pills give her vertigo, make her nauseous. She takes two pregnancy tests, doesn't tell Rob when they come up negative. She's not pregnant, just sick. That's what the doctor said. *You can manage this, just like diabetes.* She smokes cigarette after stolen cigarette. She cooks elaborate meals, picks at her food. Starts losing weight.

"What's wrong?" Rob says one night in bed after they've turned out the lights. His hand shimmies up her thigh, playing with the hem of her underwear. "You've been a wreck lately."

"More than usual, you mean."

He's noticed the pill bottles, she knows, but he hasn't asked. He'll never ask.

"I guess."

"I'm fine," she says. "I'll be fine. Let's just—" and then they're kissing, and the world goes bleak, black, blank.

She can't bring herself to say the words. *Treatment resistant.* He isn't the first psychiatrist she's seen. Not even the fifth or sixth. They all have answers, treatments, and she tries them all, no matter how sick they make her, and she still has the symptoms. The anxiety. The sleeplessness. The rages. Then the depressions. She's on a roller coaster she can't get off of, and she feels sick. She wants to go home, like a little girl who's lost her mother. But she is thirty-two, and she can't get off the ride, can't call her mother—who is dead—and no one can help her. *Take these pills.*

She does the research. ECT. Ketamine therapy. Thyroid treatments. One trip to the ER, lithium poisoning, a night spent being poked and prodded by doctors who tell her to avoid alcohol and drink more water.

She smokes another cigarette.

Dolly cleans the kitchen as Rob watches. She's like a machine, effectively wiping down surfaces. Cleaning soothes her, soothes the manic anxiety, the buzzing feeling that she talks about filling her arms and legs. Sex helps too, and he obliges, even when he's tired from working at the construction site all day. She's an odd one. They met at a party a few months ago, moved in together when his lease was up and he didn't know where to go. It's worked out. It's a pity she's crazy.

He would never say it to her face. She's a lovely girl. But she is—crazy. Chain-smoking and worried about shadows in the corners of her vision. She thinks that if she keeps a perfect house, perfect dinners, perfect martinis, perfect kitchen, it'll all go away. The perfect wife, even though they aren't married. "Babe," he said once. "You can't change the outside to change the inside. You can't domestic your-self out of this. You have to get help."

"I *am* getting help," she had said. "The help isn't help-ing."

*

She gets zapped. Short-term memory loss, but it does work, the rough edges of her mind smoothed over like concrete. For a few months, she's herself again. They talk about getting married. He picks her up and swings her around like a doll.

"I love you," she says absentmindedly over dinner, as if they've been saying it this whole time, as if it's not the first time they've ever acknowledged that this thing, this connection, is real. "Did you know that?"

"Of course, Doll," he says. "I love you too."

Rob is a good man, a port-in-a-storm kind of man. Things might be all right, he thinks to himself. She takes the pills each night, and they seem to be working. It was only a few months ago, he thinks, that she was tossing and turning in bed every night, getting up to prowl the apartment, putting gin in her water bottle to go to work. It was only a few months ago that she was maxing out their shared credit cards. Disappearing for hours only to return with strange scratches and bruises.

Now she is really the perfect woman. The woman she was always meant to be. Everything is perfect. He is happy.

The bills start coming in. $2,000 for therapy, $5,000 for the ambulance ride she took, once, for something he can't remember now, $450 for some psychiatrist; it all adds up. The ECT wasn't covered by insurance. Her insurance, through her job as an editorial assistant, doesn't cover many mental health conditions. They spend hours at the dining room table after work, trying to figure out which one of their maxed out credit cards they are going to use to pay the bills, and getting more and more frustrated and frantic.

"I don't understand," Dolly says. "I would have died without this treatment. How can it be so expensive?"

"I know, Doll," Rob says quietly. He has seen his mother go through the same thing with her cancer, and he knows the medical system isn't built to help people. He puts her $1,400 medication on his credit card that month. The next month, the card is declined.

"I need my medication," she says. "What are we going to do?"

They make it work for a few months, but eventually, there's nothing to do.

"I'm going to be crazy forever," Dolly says.

"I would never let that happen to you," Rob says. "We'll find a way."

As they slide into debt, they decide to get married. It is the happiest day of Rob's life. Dolly is manic, nervy as a racehorse, thin as a skeleton in a white dress, but she is grinning like a skull in the photos, kissing Rob on the cheek, on the mouth. They hold the ceremony at the court-house for as cheap as possible, then go to their favorite Thai place for the reception, just close friends.

"Our happy ending," Rob says, and Dolly believes him, but only for a second.

"People like me don't get happy endings," she says.

*

You have to practice acceptance, her new psychiatrist says. *You have to accept that you may always live with some degree of impairment.*

"I can't accept this," she says. "I can't live like this."

But you have to.

"I don't want to be like this anymore," Dolly says. They are having lunch in the park.

"But you have to stay," Rob says. "With me."

"I know." She takes a bite of her sandwich. "I'm not going anywhere."

"We'll make it better," he say., "I promise."

"You can't promise that."

"We'll make it something," he says. "Something good."

She looks at him, and despite everything, despite the ECT, despite the medication, despite the mental illness, despite the mania, despite being crazy, she believes him. She can't let go of hope.

It's the most normal day in existence.

Acknowledgments

I WOULD LIKE to thank the following folks without whom these stories would not have survived their early stages. With your support, these stories are making it out into the world.

Mom and Dad, duh, you're the kickstarters of this whole operation. Thanks for nothing (just kidding). Thank you for everything, and more everything, and even more everything.

Friends Anna, Nora, Casey, all of you carried me through this process, and without you I'd be lost in a swamp of rejection letters.

David Fowler, ultimate draft reader, you kick ass and take names. Thank you for all of it.

Assorted NYU professors and students who came in contact with these stories over the years, and some Eugene Lang students and professors as well; fuck you to some of you, I love you to everyone else. It's up to you who gets what.

Anyone I forgot, memory isn't my strong suit. Oh, Will, duh.

And finally, in no particular order, I'd like to thank my scattered collection of men:

Jon Perry, my NYU MFA platonic grad school husband, I love you, and your kid is going to be one well-read baby. Don't start her too early on the hard stuff, maybe try a little Cormac McCarthy before you drop her right into *Infinite Jest*. You and Liz and the lil one are so appreciated and loved.

Will, my soulmate, you are my reason for having a smartphone, because if I couldn't text you some wild ass shit at nine in the morning on Father's Day, I would have no inspiration to write about. But I'm never listening to any advice about ketamine that you ever give me—I learned that lesson the hard way.

Bill at Flexible Press, I knew you would go for it eventually; I just had to be patient! Thanks for all you do. And thank you to my wonderful pressmates, especially Elisa Sinnett and Frank Haberle, for your support and wisdom and just for being cool people. Bill really knows how to pick 'em!

Oh, and of course, Brady, you are the other half of me, and always will be. Thanks isn't a strong enough word. There isn't a word. There's just us.

About the Author

JOANNA ACEVEDO IS a writer, editor, and educator born and raised in New York City. Author of three books and two chapbooks, she works to create accessible resources for emerging writers and artists, and holds degrees from New York University, the New School, and Bard College. She lives in Brooklyn.